PIRATES OF THE DESERT

The locals call the sand dunes of the Arizona Territory southland a white ocean. One man, Barney Shivers, carries the comparison a little further when he orders his men to attack any freight shipping that he does not control, and steal the goods on board. A little old lady, Lolly Amos, contracts her nephew, Captain Parthenon Downs of the Arizona rangers, to fight back. Downs eagerly takes on the challenge — but little does he realize that his decision will draw him into a war against two bands of pirates . . .

SPECIAL MESSAGE TO READERS

THE ULVERSCROFT FOUNDATION
(registered UK charity number 264873)

was established in 1972 to provide funds for research, diagnosis and treatment of eye diseases. Examples of major projects funded by the Ulverscroft Foundation are:-

- The Children's Eye Unit at Moorfields Eye Hospital, London
- The Ulverscroft Children's Eye Unit at Great Ormond Street Hospital for Sick Children
- Funding research into eye diseases and treatment at the Department of Ophthalmology, University of Leicester
- The Ulverscroft Vision Research Group, Institute of Child Health
- Twin operating theatres at the Western Ophthalmic Hospital, London
- The Chair of Ophthalmology at the Royal Australian College of Ophthalmologists

You can help further the work of the Foundation by making a donation or leaving a legacy. Every contribution is gratefully received. If you would like to help support the Foundation or require further information, please contact:

THE ULVERSCROFT FOUNDATION
**The Green, Bradgate Road, Anstey
Leicester LE7 7FU, England
Tel: (0116) 236 4325**

website: www.foundation.ulverscroft.com

C. J. SOMMERS

PIRATES OF THE DESERT

Complete and Unabridged

LINFORD
Leicester

First published in Great Britain in 2015 by
Robert Hale Limited
London

First Linford Edition
published 2019
by arrangement with
The Crowood Press
Wiltshire

*A catalogue record for this book is available
from the British Library.*

ISBN 978–1–4448–4046–9

Published by
F. A. Thorpe (Publishing)
Anstey, Leicestershire

Set by Words & Graphics Ltd.
Anstey, Leicestershire
Printed and bound in Great Britain by
T. J. International Ltd., Padstow, Cornwall

This book is printed on acid-free paper

1

Everyone in the vicinity of Table Rock knew who Barney Shivers was. Opinion of the man was varied: some thought he was a fat, lying weasel, deserving of tar and feathers; others just knew him as a greedy, conscienceless bastard. Although these points of view were valid up to a point, his wife and dog also feared and despised him.

But Shivers was tolerated, oh was he tolerated — it was said he owned half of Arizona Territory. He did not, of course; his holdings were probably closer to an eighth of the land. He spewed gold money like a gusher when he was in a spending or bribing mood. That little touch of Midas about the man endeared him to everyone from saloon panhandlers to territorial representatives. Despised he was, but highly regarded. Money often seems to have that effect.

Those not endeared of Barney Shivers were every freighter, store owner, and customer of same in the wide territory. For Shivers had an interesting way of doing business. It had made his fortune for him and he was not going to quit now without some very strong encouragement. What Shivers was, that is, was a land pirate. There were at least five hundred freight companies within reach of Shivers's grasping hands, and maybe a dozen or so short-line carriers that had not felt the touch of his greedy fingers, these being too small or unprofitable for him to bother with, and four or five who had hired armies of guards to protect their wagons, which option cut their own profitability down close to the nub.

The usual Shivers procedure was simply to waylay a freight wagon, some of which carried up to eight tons of valuable goods destined for the Western trading posts and stores and ultimately

2

for the thousands of settlers and workmen who consumed these badly needed supplies. A mine owner might wait three months to have a pump delivered from St Louis and then find the shipment had been waylaid by Shivers. It was similarly hard on a hardware store proprietor who had to tell new settlers that he hadn't a barrel of ten-penny nails, or a housewife that she was without flour to bake her daughter's birthday cake.

Not that these items could not be found and rescued — or repurchased, if you will — but the prices were bound to be twenty-five per cent higher than they originally were and the consumer ended up paying all.

It was getting damned expensive to live and work in the Flat Rock area.

Most just grumbled and paid. After all, in the case of the mining operation, which would have to wait another few months for the proper equipment, hoping that the next shipment didn't get hijacked as well and production shut down, failure to negotiate with Shivers was unthinkable. For the local farm families and small businesses it was only a bitter pill that they had adjusted to — swallowed with much grumbling. No one moved away; they bought at higher prices; they had not come this far and suffered so much to give up now, but the rosy prospects of a new future in the West had decidedly dimmed in the shadow of Barney Shivers's depredations.

The local law was virtually impotent. The retail merchants were too disorganized. The honest freighters already operating on a shoestring, hauling leftover, weakly valued commodities over the wide expanse of wilderness land, too under-capitalized to consider hiring their own armies which would further cut into their already almost negligible profits were at a loss.

If you wanted something you bought it back from Shivers by the wagonload or purchased it from one of the Shivers-owned shops — which were starting to become numerous — at inflated prices.

Lolly Amos who had looked at the prices on five-pound sugar sacks and then thrown one bag on the floor of the store in disgust was one of the few people who would not knuckle under. Hoisting her skirts, Lolly, a sturdy, blonde woman of perhaps forty, perhaps sixty years of age, stormed out of the store, her little boots crunching sugar granules she had strewn, and over to the marshal's office, her handsome face set rebelliously. Beside the sign that read, 'Marshal's Office, Flat Rock, Arizona', the door stood open to the cool of morning. The big man with the bushy dark mustache seemed to tremble as Lolly Amos approached his desk. Samuel Keyser was not at his best with women, especially formidable women.

'Good morning, Mrs Amos,' the marshal said, making no attempt to rise. Lolly noticed that.

'I guess it would be a good morning

to you — you're pretty comfortable just sitting there, aren't you?'

'I guess I am,' Keyser said, not having a clue as to what sort of response the woman expected. His expression darkened, indicated only by a slight twitch in the long drapery of his mustache, for it was obvious that Lolly Amos had entered carrying the burden of righteous indignation. 'It's been blessedly peaceful around town lately.'

This last was said in a manner which indicated that he wished Lolly would keep things that way. She seemed disinclined.

'Do you know how much sugar sells for around Flat Rock?' Lolly demanded, her eyes dark and heated at once.

Is that what the woman had come here for? To complain about the prices at Foley's store?

'No. It's been a while since I needed to purchase any such item.' Keyser's tone was still even. Unperturbed. It was the tone of voice he usually used to defuse dangerous situations. Lolly Amos did not wish to be defused.

'It's the same with everything in this town. Folks say it's how Barney Shivers gets rich while the rest of us fashion his royal robes with our poor pennies.'

Keyser thought that was nicely put, poetic, even if it made no sense. He saw now why Lolly had come with her indignation flaring in plain sight.

'You're talking about matters that are out of my control,' Keyser said, now removing his boots from his desktop, letting them clump against the floor.

'Whose control are they under?' Lolly asked with heat. 'You know as well as I do that most of Foley's goods are what he calls 'second-market' commodities, meaning he bought them from Shivers. Goods that belonged to some freight company or other and were taken from them, under duress and sometimes by force.'

'I've heard such rumors, of course,' Marshal Keyser said, 'but what in the world do you expect me to do? The town limits are the limits of my jurisdiction. You can't expect me to ride out onto the desert and just happen to come across a freight wagon being robbed. Then what am I to do? Ride in with guns blazing against a gang of armed predators?'

Lolly placed her hands flat on Keyser's desk and leaned forward, her eyes strangely bright, intent. 'That's what my poor Mr Amos (rest his soul) would have done. The men of his time were made of sterner stuff, apparently.'

Keyser chuckled and was immediately sorry he had. He continued in his defusing voice:

'I doubt that Evan Amos would ride a fool's mission over the price of sugar. If he were not now dead and buried — '

'Thank God his time was well chosen,' Lolly said, throwing Keyser's line of argument off. 'Had he to be buried in these times we would be lucky if we could come by a tombstone to cap off his resting place — someone would have stolen it in Flat Rock these days!'

'I can see you're upset, Mrs Amos,' Marshal Keyser tried. 'If there were any way I could possibly — '

'You could! Mr Barney Shivers lives in Flat Rock, doesn't he? That places him under your jurisdiction! Why can't you arrest the man for his business activities which are said to include highway robbery?'

'Are they? Have you someone willing to swear to that in court, Mrs Amos? Allegations are the devil to prove. They'll ask how Shivers can be involved since he's here in Flat Rock at his office every day. I know — ' Marshal Keyser held up a hand, 'you'll say that everyone knows who hires the men doing the hold-ups, but can you prove it, a word of it? There are serious consequences to slander. Such unsubstantiated statements could cost you plenty — even your little farm — if they were made in court.'

Lolly was furious. 'Then you take Barney Shivers's side in this matter?'

'Mrs Amos, I don't take nobody's

9

side — such is not a part of my job. I'm just telling you that as of now with what we know for sure, and don't know, nothing can be done.'

'By you!' Lolly scoffed.

'By me,' Marshal Keyser agreed. His boots had found their way onto his desktop again.

'Well, Marshal, maybe that's just not good enough for me and the rest of the folks in this town. There may be something that can be done ... by other men not of this office.'

'Maybe so, Mrs Amos, but I don't know what and I don't know who there is that would tackle such a job. I sure don't know anybody who could handle it. Maybe you do.' This was delivered in an almost smug voice as if the marshal knew what he was talking about and the poor woman was deluded.

Maybe she was, Lolly Amos thought as she stepped out of the marshal's office into the bright morning, but she had already set her mind on a train of thought.

That was when she thought of Parthenon. Parth was a nephew of hers, of her late husband, that is. The son of Evan's sister, Gladys. Lolly struggled to recall Gladys's married name: Downs, that was it, Gladys Downs and the son was Parthenon Downs, usually called Parth, a sturdy young man Lolly had seen seldom — the last time at his Uncle Evan's funeral. He seemed a fine, respectable man unburdened by his unlikely name given to him by Gladys in one of her classical periods.

Lolly could not think of a likely playground name the other boys might have stuck him with, but she was sure there had been some — school-age boys were very inventive at that sort of game.

Yet Parthenon Downs, if he had borne a less than desirable playground name, had survived it and become a tall, strapping youngster with a soft smile and the ways of a man. Lolly had always admired the boy, vaguely envied her sister-in-law; Parth Downs was a fine gentleman, a sturdy, polite boy one

11

could always count on to try his best.

And he was an Arizona ranger.

★　★　★

The small rabbit warren in the downtown Tucson municipal building was where Captain Parthenon Downs was presently stationed. He wasn't sure if he liked this desk duty or not — it was far too new to him. The past five years had been spent quartered in private homes spread out across the territory where someone was willing to have them, or, more often, sleeping in the open country with a single blanket in all kinds of weather, eating with his fellow rangers hunched together over a small fire like any bunch of saddle-tramps and making their poor camps in the shadows of the men ahead of them — fleeing men, themselves in the shadow of a hangman's noose.

There was that and the inevitable shots fired by bushwhackers as they passed through some rough canyon or faced Parth man-to-man in some dusty street in a dying or dead desert town or in some outlaw stronghold.

No one could say a man liked that sort of work, but all had signed up for the job, willing to take the risks and the hardships.

And when you had been shot at often enough, ridden thousands of miles of rough and dangerous trails, if you survived, they promoted you, and bought you a desk, assuming that anyone would be pleased with the change of his circumstances. There was more comfort in Tucson, to be sure, more pay with the promotion, a little more prestige. They called it a soft job, and it was a plum for most of the rangers to strive for, but at times Parthenon Downs found himself feeling isolated, reading reports of a successful raid or difficult arrest, having partici- pated in none of it.

He was not alone. More than one desk jockey had given up his rank and position to return to field work — too often these men were killed not long after. Around the office it was said that it was because these rangers had gotten too old to handle the elements, the rough life, and the shooting. They had gotten tired out and rusty — the reasons they were promoted to desk jobs in the first place.

Parthenon had no opinion on these matters. To him it was just a matter of a man doing what he wished to do — or had to do. Parthenon Downs was tapping at thirty-five years of age, and he couldn't say he had missed spending twelve hours a day in the saddle, sleeping on rough ground, the lousy camp food. He now enjoyed a bed in a fair hotel, one with a bath and a barbershop, paid for by the citizens of Arizona Territory. He awoke each morning, perhaps a little stiffer, slower to unlimber his muscles, but with the near certainty of making it through the day without being shot, with a breakfast table in a neat little restaurant served by smiling women in starched dresses. It was a pleasant life, one that was supposed to be his just reward for his years of service with the rangers. It certainly wasn't the sort of comfort a man throws away mindlessly.

Still, something in a fighting man stirs when he is contacted for help.

The letter was written in a neat copperplate hand on vellum-like paper. It was long in content but especially short on details. Aunt Lolly Amos had composed it and spent quite a bit of time inquiring as to his health; did he remember her and the little parties they used to have when the children were little? All that sort of chatter a person with few contacts can store up over the years. It was all very polite of Aunt Amos, but really meant little after all this time.

Until she began to tell him about Barney Shivers and the land pirates.

2

It didn't take a lot of intelligence to find the hijacked wagon; what it did require was a lot of patience.

Using a compass at his office desk, Parthenon had inscribed circles at ten and twenty miles from the town of Flat Rock, the reasonable distances a ten-ton freight wagon with a six- or eight-horse team could be expected to travel before it needed to stop for water. The country to the west, of course, was excluded due to the Yavapai Mountains over which expanse no wagon could be driven — and where would a prize have originated in that direction? Waterholes were always indicated on ranger maps where they were known to exist, but Parth knew from first-hand experience that those seen one year might not be there the next, leaving only a sun-baked crater behind to mark their former existence.

Besides, he was looking for some-place that had water in abundance — those horse teams required much fresh water. Within the twenty-mile circle Parth had drawn on his map was one place he knew well. It had the rather unappealing name of Vulture Hole, but Parth had been there in his wandering days and it was a pleasant little place for a traveling man in the desert to come upon. A grove of sycamore trees crowded the ridge and there was the usual stand of willow brush decorating the basin, which seemed to have a water source beneath the desert floor.

That would be the place — a place for Parthenon to begin his search.

His supervisor was Arizona Ranger Superintendent Gabriel Lindquist, a fussy little sharp-eyed man with more scars on his body from the rigors of his work than could be counted.

'I hate to see you leaving, Parth,' was what he had said when Parthenon told his him what he intended to do.

Parthenon was at his own desk, checking the loads in his revolver. Lindquist stood in the doorway, not quite frowning, 'Over five pounds of sugar.'

'That's not it, Gabriel, and you know it. These hijackers are running free in the West and there are thousands of people hurt by their piracy.'

'That's a large job for one man to take on,' Lindquist replied. 'Are you sure you're up to it?' he asked, perhaps thinking of the others who had tried to return to the field after a stint of office work and found themselves coming up short.

'I've kept my guns oiled,' Parthenon said, rising. 'And if I need more help, I guess I know where to ask for it.'

'Yes, and you won't have to wait long for it if you bring back solid evidence, something a little larger than your aunt's sugar bag.'

'It's there to be found, Gabriel,' Parthenon said, believing it. 'It's just that no one has gone looking for it before.'

'You're likely to find trouble first,' Lindquist said. He then offered his scaly hand to Parthenon Downs. They shook hands without another word. Then the superintendent disappeared into the interior of the office building.

Parthenon discovered quickly that what Lindquist and others had told him was true. A long day on the desert beneath a smelter-hot sun had him more than ready to take his rest at Vulture Hole by the time he reached it. Outside of Sunday rides, Parthenon had spent little time in the saddle for a long time. He felt like a tenderfoot by the time he swung down, his inner thighs aching, his head spinning with sun spots after a day of staring at the glaring white sand.

Vulture Hole seemed like Mecca. After watering his horse and filling his canteens, he withdrew a little into the sycamore trees where he could clearly see the springs but anyone arriving

19

would need a sharp eye to see him. The horse, a big gray he had owned for years, munched contentedly on the bright green grass there, and after settling at the base of a tree, Parthenon found himself feeling comfortable enough to take a nap in the shade. But he did not: he was afraid of missing any visitors to the watering hole which he was sure must lie along the route of any freighter, legal or outlaw.

As the sun began to drop toward the distant Yavapai Mountains, coloring the sky and sand alike, Parthenon's patience was rewarded. The six-horse team pulled the wagon slowly toward the water hole, as if the driver were surveying his surroundings carefully. Probably he was. The wagon was a modified Conestoga and not one of those monster fifteen-foot long freighters like those that Studebaker built. These carried nine tons of merchandise in a light load — that would have been a lot of profit to trust to a single driver. So was whatever this man carried.

He could be transporting anything and everything from a child's hoped-for Christmas toy to a housewife's badly needed iron skillet. All the tools and furnishings for a house had to be freighted out here — to nowhere from somewhere — and the freighters themselves were lionized for other things than their prodigious drinking, always on display at trail's end: they faced Indians, bandits, and the roughest roads ever to be carved across the land. The freighters Parthenon had met were all tough, grizzled, and good with their guns.

Now these tough, honest men were also having to deal with hijackers: land pirates who faced no difficulties of their own other than learning how to point a Colt at another man.

And which sort was the lone approaching waggoner? There was only one way to find out. Parthenon rose, took a knife to his woven saddle cinch and cut through it: no matter — he rode always with a spare in his saddlebags. Then he led the bemused gray back toward the water hole.

He could hear the wagon drawing nearer; at least one of its axle hubs needed greasing.

Experienced freighters rarely let necessary maintenance like that go; their wagons were their livelihood; a breakdown could mean their lives.

For someone having only one use for the wagon, to transport stolen goods, maintenance was not an issue. It was a dead giveaway that the man approaching Vulture Hole had been up to no good.

There was no point in hesitating. Parthenon thought that the worst thing he could do was to appear unannounced out of the trailside brush; that was bound to bring a violent response. The man, whoever he was, was likely running afraid, certainly vigilant of the law and other thieves as well. There were men along these distant trails who would shoot you down for an iron pot — those being rare and far between in the land of the Indian, and in Mexico as well. All these people could craft an *olla* well and quickly, but these clay pots did not wear well and had to be replaced at every campsite.

Parthenon stepped forward with his rifle dangling in his hand, his arm upraised. The driver of the Conestoga reached first for the Winchester riding in the boot of his wagon, then peered into the late sunlight at Parthenon, his expression suspicious, uncertain. It was left to Parthenon Downs to begin the conversation.

'Howdy, friend! I'm glad to see someone away out here. I can only hope that you're heading for Flat Rock or somewhere near.' Parth walked forward trying to look friendly and a little simple. The wagon driver's eyes did not waver. 'I broke a cinch strap back away, and I'm due in Flat Rock. I hate the thought of walking all that way, or even worse, riding that bronc of mine bareback. I can tell you, he don't have no easy pace, and — '

'The company don't allow us to take no riders,' the driver said sharply.

'No? That seems kind of a cruel policy in this country. You ever been afoot in this desert, friend? I didn't get your name.' Parthenon was now near enough to the wagon that he could place his hand on the heated flank of the near horse.

'The name's Bob Brown,' the driver said hesitantly.

'That's an easy name to remember,' Parthenon answered. And an easy one to produce.

'Bob, there's still plenty of cool water ahead and good graze. Let me help you with the team.'

'Don't need any help, don't want any help,' the narrow, beady-eyed man who chose to call himself Bob Brown, said. Well, he did, Parthenon knew. It was a real job to unharness and water six horses, each of them wanting to be first to quench its thirst. One reason why a swamper was an integral part of a well-run wagon team. Another point

24

that made Parthenon more than suspicious of Mr Brown, who traveled alone.

Brown started the team forward toward the water-hole, Parthenon walking at his side. Once they had passed through the scattered shade of the cottonwood trees, Parthenon spoke up, 'That rear hub is still squealing pretty good.'

'It'll be all right,' Brown said indicating with his tone that it was none of Parth's business.

'What are you running back there?' Parthenon asked. 'Boxing and skein?'

Brown's face showed nothing but angry ignorance. He didn't know, obviously. Maybe he even had no idea that that was a common sort of hub arrangement. That settled it for Parth — the man was only a catch-as-catch-can driver, not a freighter by profession.

Reining and braking his six-horse team to a halt, Brown clambered down and went to the water first. Parthenon left the man to himself for the moment and went to retrieve his stage setting

— the saddle with the broken cinch strap, mud rubbed on its ends to camouflage the recent knife cut. His gray horse followed him back to the waterhole and drank what it wanted as the wagon team watched indignantly. It was an odd team, Parthenon was thinking; five bay horses and one black. Perhaps the black was not a part of the wagon's original team. He mentioned nothing about that.

'Partner,' he said to Mister Brown, 'I surely need to get to Flat Rock, and you seem to be going that way, how about a little trail mercy? I don't know you, I don't know your bosses, whoever they are. I'm certainly not going to tell anyone that you did so, if you'd be kind enough to give me a lift. I've people waiting for me there.'

'What kind of people?' Brown asked, his suspicion still evident.

'My wife and mother,' Parthenon invented, 'my little boy.' He watched Bob Brown going about his own business. Family troubles like these were obviously not going to sway him.

'I could pay you for the ride,' Parthenon tried. Brown looked up sharply.

'How much?' he asked, his eyes dully glittering.

'All I have in this world is twenty-five dollars. I guess I can go as high as ten gold dollars for a lift. It's most important that I get to town.'

Ten dollars wasn't much to a man who had a wagonload of valuable cargo, but Brown had not sold that yet — and the cargo was not his. To be caught chipping at the gang's profits as he seemed to be doing was to find himself in big trouble, Parthenon guessed. As for the wagon itself, no one knew and no one would care where it came from. Ten easy cash dollars was not to be sneezed at.

'All right,' Bob Brown said as if he were experiencing martyrdom. 'Ten bucks now — in cash. You can hitch your pony up behind, then help me with this miserable team of mine.'

'Sure thing, Bob,' Parthenon said with eager gratitude. Then he fished a ten-dollar gold piece from his jeans and placed it in Brown's sweaty palm. The gray horse he tied on behind the wagon before he climbed up into the box where Brown's rifle still rested near his knee. Looking up he could see the wagon driver fussing with a difficult harness latch. Brown was standing in the middle of the water, the balky black horse refusing to settle and help him in any way. Parthenon picked up the team's reins and kicked off the standing brake.

'I'll draw them back a little, Bob! Far enough so that you have dry ground to stand on.'

'No you don't!' Bob Brown yelled. 'Don't you touch those reins! I told you I don't need no help, and I don't — Hey, what are you doing?'

What Parthenon Downs was doing was backing up the horse team as an angry Brown fought toward the shore, slipping on the muddy pond bottom.

By the time Brown had his feet firmly planted on dry ground, he could only watch as Parthenon turned the team and lit out for the open desert in his wagon. Mr Brown then proceeded to add a few new entries to the dictionary of profanity.

★   ★   ★

Parthenon Downs was riding high, wide, and handsome when he turned the horse team onto Shuttle Road leading to his Aunt Lolly's farm — if it could be called a farm still as the land hadn't been properly worked since Uncle Evan had died. Lolly told the folks who were interested that she was only letting the land lie fallow. Parth doubted the woman had the strength and determination to bring the farm back to what it had once been. How old was Lolly now? Parthenon knew she had reached the last birthday she would acknowledge, years ago. When she was dressed up for Sunday she didn't look to be over forty or thereabouts, but watching her in his younger days, as she moved about, there was a hitch to her gait and the hesitation that argued that her middle years had progressed into old age. And he had not seen her in years.

Nevertheless, the sight of the little ranch nestled in the valley with a few scattered white oaks surrounding it made Parthenon's spirits rise — it was a little bit like coming home from some distant war.

There were still some lights in the low white house, one in front, another at the rear, and when the big Conestoga wagon rumbled into the yard and was braked to a halt, there came scurrying, excited sounds from within. Parthenon knew that he should have gone directly to the Flat Rock marshal's office, but it was important to him that his aunt know that when she called on Parthenon Downs for help, by God, she was going to get it.

The curtains across the front window

were drawn back a few inches, then the front door to the little house was flung wide and a small woman in a dark blue house dress emerged to stand, arms akimbo, peering up at Parthenon in the dark night.

'Parthenon Downs, is that you!' Lolly Amos shouted. 'Well, it took you long enough.'

'I caught the first coach I could find,' Parthenon joked.

'I see that,' Lolly said as he stepped down from the box. Eyeing the tarpaulin cargo the wagon carried, she asked with mock sternness, 'You didn't forget my sugar, did you?'

'You know, I really haven't taken the time to look yet,' Parthenon answered.

'Just like a man; you send him to a store to get one thing and he comes back with everything but that single item!' Then, as Parth's feet hit the ground, Lolly came to him and embraced him tightly.

'You're a dear boy; thank you for coming.'

The dust was still sifting in from Parth's arrival and he glanced down the road, not expecting that he had been followed, but simply exercising prudent caution. 'I'll need to water the horses, and . . . ' he began, and then he saw her behind the veil of dust like an actress on stage appearing behind a gauze curtain.

Young she was, with a flow of auburn hair trickling across her shoulders and breasts, mouth compressed with cautious uncertainty. Her eyes were wide and blue, but still, as if she did not wish to open herself up to anyone. Aunt Lolly glanced at Parthenon, who had frozen in his motion. Then she glanced across her shoulder at the apparition and smiled, taking Parthenon's arm at the shoulder.

'Come along, Parthenon. Let me introduce you — this is Sally Shields. She's been staying with me for a while, helping me out with my chores.

'That's fine,' Parthenon Downs said, smiling and offering his hand to Sally.

She looked at him as if astonished by the gesture, turned away and left, her eyes fixed on him until she entered the haven of the house.

'Don't pay any attention to Sally's ways,' Parth's aunt told him. 'The girl's had a rough time of it and it's left her a little shy.'

'Of everyone, or just men?'

'She's a little shy,' was all Aunt Lolly would answer. The look Parthenon had caught in the girl's eyes was not fear exactly, but they had expressed extreme wariness. Well, he decided, that attribute could be beneficial to someone who was into something she didn't totally understand.

He continued to gaze at the closed door where Sally had vanished until Aunt Lolly swung a hip in his direction, nudging him. 'Better see to this collection of ponies you've brought along with you, then I'll make you some fresh coffee and you can sample that crumb cake I've just taken from the oven.'

Not being familiar with the team or their harness, it took some time for him to water the beasts, loose them into the empty corral behind the house, and return, rapping loudly on the door frame before entering, his hat now removed.

Before he had even entered the small, yellow-painted kitchen, he could smell the rich dark coffee and fresh crumb cake. Aunt Lolly had an apron on now and hovered near the stove, putting butter on the cake. Sally Shields was there as well, standing near the open back door, but when she turned and caught a look at Parthenon, she brushed past him and left the kitchen, the leather heels of her tiny boots clacking away down the hallway.

'Find my sugar?' Lolly asked without turning.

'I haven't had a chance to check over the goods yet.'

'Well, don't blame me if the cake doesn't come up to your expectations, Parthenon. I couldn't wait forever for you to show up with my sugar.' She wiped her hands on a small dish towel with embroidered red flowers on it, and grew serious.

'How much trouble are you in now?'

3

Aunt Lolly's question was still unanswerable the following morning.

Parthenon had no idea how much trouble he might have stirred up; it was certain that someone would be unhappy with having three tons of merchandise taken from him. What it would do, at worst, was bring the land pirates out into the open. At the present these men, whoever they were, sailed the bleak seas of sands, unnoticed until they raised their piratical flags of warning, and once their intentions were understood, the freighters yielded almost immediately to the skull and crossbones, giving up their land galleons and golden cargo without a shot having been fired. The men of the sandy seas had come to an understanding about these affairs long ago. Few men were willing to fight for goods which were not even their own as opposed to surrendering and staying alive.

All of that was understandable: the land ships carried no deck cannon and the men who had been hired as freighters had their lives and families to consider. There was no willingness on the part of these men to watch their own blood being spilled for someone else's merchandise.

A group of heavily armed men could approach these wagons and politely ask that the galleon-sized load of merchandise be abandoned, provide a new wagon driver and vanish across the desert sea, leaving the freighters effectively marooned.

Parthenon Downs let his mind ramble among these and other thoughts as he guided the six-horse team pulling the loaded wagon toward Flat Rock on this clear, sun-bright desert day.

These conjectures were only occasionally interrupted with concern over the sad-eyed, red-headed girl, Sally

Shields. Who was she, where had she come from? Both of the women had been asleep that morning when Parthenon went out into the cool dawn to harness the horses, and so he had not had the time to ask Lolly any more questions about the shy bird who was Sally Shields.

He rolled in along the dusty main street of Flat Rock just as the colors of the eastern sky were at their most sublime, having spread a palette of crimson and violet above the white desert landscape. The marshal's office was not hard to find with the aid of a passing schoolboy, books bound for his walk to class.

It was still too early for the marshal to be at his desk, however; Parthenon figured the man to be at a local café having a last, lingering cup of coffee. The idea sounded appealing to him as well, but he was not about to leave the shipment untended in the street. He killed some time by untying the tarp and searching the shipping labels on the goods he had rescued. There was a small fortune in merchandise and some longed-for necessities on this wagon alone.

But no sugar, he noticed. Parthenon stopped a passing teenage boy and gave him a dime to take his gray over to the stable, then he settled in to wait for Marshal Keyser.

★   ★   ★

Marshal Sam Keyser stepped from the Faerie Plum restaurant into the brilliant morning light, his stomach's needs satisfied, the town at this hour peaceful and quiet. That was just the way he liked things. Keyser needed no extra excitement in his life. Leave the hell-raising to those who were cut out for it, and let those men leave him alone. As a younger man he had posted himself in front of outlaws with his gun at the ready. It was a good way to get shot, as he had discovered.

On this morning he strolled contentedly toward his office with Effie True's good breakfast riding comfortably in his stomach. The English woman had named her restaurant improbably: The Faerie Plum. It didn't matter to him what she called it as long as her coffee was hot and the pies she made out of dried apples were piping in the restaurant ovens, filling the place with that pleasant cinnamon and sugar scent he appreciated.

Keyser asked Effie True only once why she had given her restaurant that name after he had gotten to know her. Her answer was succinct and unenlightening: 'There's little enough to feed the souls of this maddening desert.'

Keyser had pondered that for a while and then shrugged it away — if Effie True was a little touched in the head, it didn't bother anyone in the community.

Nearing his office, Marshal Keyser hoped he would not run into the unpleasant Jarrett Taylor on this morning. Taylor had lost his prized jenny mule and come to the office about it. Keyser had promised to help in the search, but effectively he had given up on the idea before he had begun. He couldn't be expected to ride the hard, dry land searching for a mule. Taylor had lost it; let him find it.

There was no sign of Taylor's squat bay horse in front of the office — that was for the good.

However, rather surprisingly, when Keyser arrived there was a Conestoga wagon loaded to the limit with trade goods. A trim, dark-haired man stood beside it, smiling vaguely as he watched the marshal's slow approach. Keyser's face was already quizzical, then, as he came within a few strides, still not recognizing Parthenon, he demanded in that way of those usually isolated from the world:

'Just who are you and what are you doing here?'

Parthenon had reached into his jeans pocket and he now handed the marshal his five-pointed rangers' badge with

41

'Captain' inscribed on it. Keyser studied the badge for a long minute as if it meant nothing to him, or if it did he was sorry to be seeing it. He looked again at Parthenon Downs, again at the wagon, handed back the badge and said, 'Come on inside.'

They had barely made it through the marshal's door when Keyser removed his hat, hung it on a wall peg and asked, 'Does this have anything to do with the price of sugar?'

Parthenon grinned. The man had met his Aunt Lolly, then. The marshal allowed himself a small smile as he settled back behind his desk.

'You've guessed it,' Parthenon said. Keyser shook his head as if it weighed too much for his neck to support.

'I might have known that ignoring that woman would do no good, the mood she was in.' He began drumming his fingers on his desktop. 'Mind telling me what brings you here, and with that freight wagon?'

'The whole business with these land

pirates,' Parthenon said, finding a straight-backed chair to sit on. 'It's not just Flat Rock that they're affecting, but all of the territory. Tucson is interested in finding these raiders.'

'Meaning you . . . or the rangers?'

'It's the same thing. What is a five-pound sack of sugar to one person is thousands of dollars in machinery to a copper mine when it's needed. You have to know that as well as I do.'

'I guess so,' Keyser said. He looked a little uncomfortable now. Maybe he had gotten into the habit of ignoring the entire business, felt uneasy thinking about it. Maybe it was just too big for him. 'So you were sent down to take a look at matters, is that it?'

'That's it. Although I have to admit that I was the one initiating this grand plan.'

'On behalf of Lolly Amos.'

'Mostly.'

'Ah, the power of a woman,' Keyser muttered. He seemed to be smiling still though it was difficult to tell behind the screen of his thick, dark mustache.

'Yes, well it seemed the time was ripe for investigation,' Parthenon answered in explanation.

'How'd you get to be a captain in the rangers?' Marshal Keyser asked as if he were trying to sidetrack the conversation.

'Oh, you know how it is, Marshal. The same as in the army. You just stick around long enough and someone's going to figure that if you've been there that long, you probably deserve to be promoted.'

Keyser continued to drum on his desktop. He looked up sharply and said, 'I would guess what that means is that you have done your share of fighting for the outfit over a stretch of time.'

'However you want to state it,' Parthenon said in a way which indicated his record was a matter of indifference to him. 'I'm more concerned with the present and what you can tell me about Barney Shivers and

44

the land pirates.'

'I probably don't know anything you don't know already,' Keyser said, tilting back in his chair as if settling into a long tale. 'But I can give you a little background:

'Barney Shivers drifted into Flat Rock over twenty years ago when there wasn't nothing here but snakes and two or three of the earliest settlers — like your aunt and uncle. Other folks eventually started to come in, due to our good ground-water situation, and as soon as these folks made the trek in, they started needing goods — everything from a needle and thread to plows, long underwear, and beans. I mean everything.

'Barney Shivers saw the light of profit, and he was a man with a few bucks he had made somewhere else — how, I couldn't guess — and he bought a few of the Conestoga wagons the settlers had arrived in, refitted them and started making early runs to the railhead in Phoenix where he shopped for the cheapest goods he could find — damaged goods and items that had been over-ordered a lot of the time. He didn't give a damn if folks liked his shoddy merchandise or not — his motto was, 'Let them buy or do without'.

'That's where Shivers's reputation began to go on the downslide. All of the early settlers knew Shivers and refused to deal with him if there was an alternative — but there weren't many other ways to go to purchase what a person needed.'

'He had a corner on the market in the early days,' Parthenon put in.

'You could say that!' Keyser answered with a laugh. 'What he had was an iron-clad monopoly. Now and then people would get frustrated and a few of them tried to start up little bootstrap freight lines. They couldn't hardly compete. Shivers had all his sources sewed up, and the only goods the new freight lines were able to haul in were cast-offs, and the prices were no cheaper. People went back to Barney Shivers. He, at least, delivered the goods, the pirate.'

Marshal Keyser paused, taking in a deep breath. There was some sort of ruckus back in the jail cells, and Keyser glanced that way but did not rise.

'I'm taking up a lot of your time,' Parthenon said.

'No matter — the boys back there are just angry about breakfast being late. They'll have to wait until one of my deputies shows up. My regular prisoners know that. It must be a couple of first-timers acting up. Can't seem to convince them that jail is not where you get room service.

'It's nothing new, Captain. I've been listening to these same complaints for twelve years now.'

'Long time to be on the same job.'

'It is.' Keyser leaned forward, smiled and said, 'Don't tell no one, Captain, but I happen to like this job. Now then, we were discussing Barney Shivers.

'A few of these new shoestring

freighters were stubborn, one man in particular named Golden Loggins, and after a while he was even showing a small profit. Tough kid, he was ... Anyway, that was about when Shivers must have made his decision — this was three, four years ago. He had been making a lot of money, but apparently it wasn't enough for him, and he considered that he was doing all the work. I think in his own mind he actually believed he had given the young freighters their start, following in his tracks.'

'About then, you say, he decided he was doing things the hard way,' Parthenon Downs said. He was interrupted.

'It seems so — Shut up back there! You'll be fed soon enough. If you wanted early breakfast you shouldn't have gotten yourself into trouble last night!' Keyser smiled an apology at Parthenon.

'That won't do any good,' he said. 'Where do these young roisterers get the idea that the law owes them since they are in our custody?' Keyser shook his head, perhaps thinking of the old days when he would have just gone back to the cells and cracked a few heads. Maybe he would have done that now if he had not had company.

'You were saying Shivers started to change his business practices,' Parthenon prompted.

Marshal Keyser exhaled loudly, lifting the hairs of his black mustache. 'He did. I started to notice that he wasn't running as many wagons out as formerly. I thought maybe the new freighters had given him too much competition and that maybe Barney Shivers was tapering down his business, maybe thinking of retirement.'

'But he wasn't.'

'No sir. What he was actually doing, it seems, was expanding his concerns. I never had any proof of it, you see. In the beginning I'd see two or three rough-looking men hanging around Shivers's freight yard, like drifters hoping to be hired on. They'd be around town for a day or two, spending their nights in the hotel on Shivers's dollar — I know, I checked that out — and then they'd be gone. The next week there'd be a few more tough-appearing sorts repeating the same pattern.'

'Did you ever talk to any of them?'

'A couple of times. There was no point in it; they all had the same story; they were looking for a job.'

'It seems they found one.'

'It seems they did,' Keyser admitted. 'From all I know, and some I don't know, they got jobs as cargo rustlers. I don't know where their camp is — somewhere on that godforsaken desert, but they know when a wealthy ship-ment is due in.'

'I guess that would be no problem, with Shivers's connections.'

'No. And after a while someone will ride in having discovered the stolen shipments and Shivers will go on to reclaim them and return them to the original owners — for a substantial finder's fee.'

'And people have to pay up,' Parthenon said.

'Pay or never see the shipment again. Shivers doesn't care either way: he can sell the goods somewhere else or stock them in his own stores.'

'This is all pretty blatant, it seems to me,' Parthenon commented.

'It is, but folks have come to understand that this is the way business is conducted out here. The risk is figured into their prices. It's generally accepted as being no more than a sort of toll-road tax; everybody pays it.'

'And the price of everything keeps going up.'

'Yes, even on sugar,' the marshal said, allowing himself another small smile.

Parthenon got to his feet, picking up his hat. The marshal also rose. 'There's something else, Captain?'

'A few things. Do you have the time to come out to the wagon? Most of the merchandise I have still has shipping labels on it. I can return it to the parties it was intended for. And I'd like to ask you about a man named Bob Brown.

'Lastly, I'll need directions to the home of Barney Shivers.'

The marshal looked briefly stunned. 'I wouldn't go out there, Captain. It could mean a lot of trouble for you.'

'I imagine it could, but Barney Shivers is the man behind all of this, a fact everyone seems to know; it only makes sense for me to interview him, wouldn't you say?'

'I would say,' Marshal Keyser said as they stepped out into the sunlight and went to the rear of the stolen wagon, 'that it's the only way you have a chance to complete your investigation, but I have to repeat what I told you before. I wouldn't go out there, Captain. It could mean a whole lot of trouble for you if you talk to Barney Shivers. Blood trouble.'

4

With the help of one of Keyser's deputies, a sour-looking man named Cather, Parthenon was able to deliver almost all of the goods to their originally intended recipients, all of whom were expansively happy to receive the long-given up on merchandise.

The hotel was especially relieved. A small business run by a Dutchman and his round little wife, they had spent all of their time and money building up the place, which was not exactly located at a Western center of commerce.

'So we spend all we have and are ready to open!' the Dutchman said. 'There can be no delays now, but there was a big one. No mattresses! How are people supposed to come here to stay? I thank you so much, Mister Captain,' he was saying as a dozen new mattresses were unloaded by the hotel crew, which from appearances were all members of the Dutchman's family.

'You ever need a place to stay — for you, it is free,' the hotel owner said.

Parthenon wondered again how many lives must be affected across the territory in so many ways by the land pirates.

'You sure made him happy,' Deputy Cather said. He seemed like someone who had never been happy in his life and did not intend to start now. His dour face indicated no willingness to even try experimenting with such an emotion. There are such men.

'All right,' Parthenon said as the two walked back to the front of the wagon, 'we've got about a dozen barrels on board bound for a place called Placer's Dance Hall. Know where that is?'

'Don't I? I spend as much time there breaking up fights as some other men do drinking.'

'It does a good business, then?'

'Does it not! And if those are whiskey

barrels back there as I think, they'll be glad as Christmas to see you.'

'That cargo could have been turned over quickly by the pirates, I'd think,' Parthenon said, thinking out loud.

'Couldn't it,' Cather agreed. 'That's what Barney Shivers sets his eyes on — high profit items with a quick turnover.'

'I can see that. An establishment like Placer's would be willing to pay twice what the whiskey is worth if they were close to running out and knew the alternative was just to close down their place of business.'

'Or make their own liquor,' Cather said as if that were not beyond the saloonkeeper. 'Second alley to your left. I assume we want the loading dock and not a front door arrival.'

'That seems the prudent alternative,' Parthenon agreed with a grin. Cather was not amused. Nothing amused him. Maybe he had a bad tooth troubling him; more likely it was his natural disposition.

Parthenon was welcomed like a prodigal son once he explained why he had come to Placer's Dance Hall. The owner, a man named Dwight Charles, was a narrow man in a black suit, the inflections of the South in his voice. By the time the whiskey barrels were unloaded, Parthenon was being treated as warmly as a favorite brother.

'Any time you want to pay us a visit, maybe get introduced to one of our hostesses, leave your purse at home, Captain — your money's no good at Placer's.'

Charles was practically clinging to Parthenon, his face red with exultant relief as they said goodbye, shaking hands.

'That hearty warmth surprised me,' Cather said. 'You ought to see the way Charles treats any man who can't pay in his place.'

'Well, I did the man a favor — doing so will always carry you along for a day or two. Not that long if you actually expect to be paid back.'

'I guess you're right,' Cather muttered, tugging his hat down against the glare of the mid-morning sun. 'What's left to deliver back there?' Parthenon asked, nodding his head toward the back of the wagon.

'It looks like most of it belongs to Foley — his store's along this way towards Main Street. Mostly it seems to be hand tools, which a few folks around here will be pleased to see come in.'

The wagon was taken to the rear alley at Foley's store. Foley himself, a round man with just enough hair on his skull to indicate that he had once had a crop growing there emerged from the store, his faced wreathed in smiles. He looked the two lawmen over and said, 'Finally got here, did it! Fine, fine!'

'Get your men to climb up and unload everything that's got your packing slip on it, will you?' Cather asked. As the day grew warmer so did the deputy's temperature. 'I've got other duties than going around playing

Santa Claus, you know.'

He walked away grumbling; Foley paid him no mind. 'He's always just a little like that,' the shopkeeper told Parthenon. He nodded with satisfaction as his workers unloaded the wagon. Foley stood by with an ordering invoice, stopping the men now and then to check an article more closely.

'Well there may be an item or two missing,' Foley said when they had finished, 'but perhaps that was my error — I'll have to double-check. I'll tell you what, though, I'm mighty happy to have gotten this load. You have no idea how some of the men around here can get when I haven't a hammer, saw, or axe I've promised.'

'I can imagine. They need tools to work, and they want to get to work.'

'Yes, I know,' Foley said almost solemnly. He was checking the wagon bed one last time. 'What's that?'

'Looks like a pair of work boots to me. Size eleven? Can I leave those with you too, shipping tag or not?'

'I don't remember anyone ordering those.'

'Keep them anyway — when he's down to walking so that he can feel every pebble, he'll be back. Think how pleased he'll be not to have to buy another pair.'

'I suppose that's the best way. Captain, can I do anything for you? You've saved me an almighty lot of work and money today.'

'Maybe one thing,' Parthenon answered. 'Do you happen to know a woman named Lolly Amos?'

'Do I not!' the shopkeeper laughed, then his expression sobered. He studied Parthenon intently.

'What about her?'

'If you'd like to pay me back for my trouble would you just please make sure that she can buy her sugar from you at last year's price?'

Foley agreed to that simple, low-cost compromise and promised Parthenon as he stepped back into the Conestoga's box. 'Anytime you need something

59

— at cost — just come around, Captain.'

'I'll do that,' Parthenon answered. Cather was not included in the offer, but the deputy looked as if he had not expected any such gesture.

'I need to get back and check in with the marshal,' Cather said as they pulled out onto the dusty, white main street of town.

'That's where I was planning on going right now.'

Cather looked momentarily abashed, 'I mean, you don't need no help with the horses and wagon, do you?'

Parthenon was able to reassure the deputy. 'No, that'll be fine. I thank you, but I'm going to leave the job to the hostler. He's used to such work.'

'Is that where you're going — the stable?'

'I've got to,' Parthenon said as they drew up in front of the marshal's office. 'That's where my own pony is, and I've got no use for a six-horse team. Maybe Marshal Keyser can figure out who they belong to by the stable records and brands. Someone would be pleased to have them back.'

'I'll say,' Cather commented, stepping down to the ground. He eyed the weary team again. 'I could almost swear I'd seen these horses somewhere before, I can't remark where, though I can tell you for certain that that black horse wasn't mixed in with them then.'

'No — he's definitely the odd one. I imagine they used it to replace the one they shot dead to stop this wagon, wouldn't you?'

Cather looked again at the black, patted the rump of the near bay, then with a shrug and a muttered farewell he stepped up onto the porch and tramped into the marshal's office to report and return to his regular duties. A second deputy, younger, rail thin, wearing a black hat with an extremely wide brim, glanced out of the office at Parthenon and then closed the door.

Parthenon started the team toward the stables.

The man in charge was short, one-eyed, and dressed nearly in rags. Parthenon asked him on a chance, 'Do you happen to know a man named Bob Brown?' The stable hand laughed out loud. Parthenon just studied the man, waiting for the fit of amusement to die down.

'You're not long in Flat Rock, I take it. Mister, it seems we must have had some sort of epidemic in naming babies some years ago. I swear every fourth man drifting through town lately is named Bob Brown. John Smith must have moved on.'

'A common alias for wandering men, is it?'

'Common as fleas on a dog,' the stable hand answered. 'What is it you've brought me, Mister . . . ?'

'The name is Downs,' Parthenon said. 'What I've brought is that team and wagon out front. The five bays and the black, along with that Connie wagon they're pulling. Marshal Keyser knows I've brought them here — I suppose the town will be paying for their keep. They were stolen from someone, I suspect, but that doesn't mean they don't deserve water, feed, and a decent rub down.'

'Wait a minute — I'm not sure I want to get involved with stolen horses,' the one-eyed man said shakily.

'Send someone to talk to the marshal if you're unsure. The horses are no longer stolen; they're found. The worst that can happen to you is you end up with six nice horses and a Conestoga, costing you little more than your time and some feed.'

'Mister, this is Flat Rock, I could end up having my head shot off by their original owner. You'd better find some-place else to take this rig.'

'Hell of a way to talk to strangers,' said a soft baritone voice from the open double doors of the stable. 'Besides, those are my horses, and I haven't shot your head off yet, have I, Marvin?'

'Mr Loggins!' the stable hand said with obvious relief. He had worked himself into a tizzy trying to make a decision about the stolen team and wagon.

The man who stepped into the darkness of the stable's interior from the brilliant sunlight beyond its doors was younger than Parthenon, dressed in a neat pearl-gray suit and black ribbon tie. He was around six feet tall, well set up. His blond hair was neatly barbered, his face clean-shaven. He wore a gold pinkie ring and a single, low-slung Colt with mother-of-pearl grips. Parthenon was quick to take in these small points: that was a part of his life — identifying and sizing up a man.

'Are you Parthenon Downs?' the stranger asked, stepping toward them with an easy stride. He proffered a hand. 'I was just now talking to Marshal Keyser about you. Did you have much trouble reclaiming the wagon?'

'Nothing much to talk about.'

'Mind telling me who you recovered

it from?' Golden Loggins asked. Parthenon shook his head, understanding now that it was a common local alias for Flat Rock men who were unwilling to own up to another name.

'I found a man named Bob Brown traveling alone out near Vulture Hole. We had a very small disagreement about the matter — I imagine he's walking this way as we speak, having no other place to go.'

'Not if he had taken a notion to go solo against the Shivers gang — a foolish or desperate move.'

'Men tend to get both foolish and desperate where money is concerned,' Parthenon said. Then he proceeded to give Loggins and Marvin a description of the man he knew as Bob Brown.

'That could be old Reliance Havens,' Loggins said, glancing at Marvin, who agreed.

'It sounds like him, I knew he was working for Shivers. I don't know what would make him go crazy enough to cross the big man.'

'Who knows?' Loggins replied. 'There could be fifty reasons. All I know is it turned out lucky for me that he did — and that he happened to run into the ranger here. Will you check the ponies over, Marvin; see that they are all branded proper with my company mark?'

'There'll be one that isn't,' Parthenon said. 'There's an unmatched black running with the team. My first thought was that he's a replacement horse for one that was shot to stop the wagon.'

'You're probably right,' Loggins said. 'I'll check them all.' He smiled, 'Although that wasn't the way I was planning on spending my afternoon.'

'No. Look, Loggins, when you have the time I'd like to talk to you about Barney Shivers.'

'Sure. All right; if I can think of any way to describe him that uses more than four letters. But not today,' he said consulting his watch. 'As I said I have a pretty full schedule for this afternoon. Come around some other time, this evening if you like — anyone can point you toward where I live.'

Golden Loggins nodded and strode out after slipping the stableman some hard money for taking care of his wagon and team. The young blond man seemed to be getting along pretty well. Why hadn't Shivers crushed him? Possibly it was because they both lived in Flat Rock and it would be too obvious. Probably, although Loggins seemed prosperous enough, he was small potatoes to Shivers and hardly worth bothering with.

Taking up the reins to his gray horse once again, Parthenon stepped out into the brilliant light of the desert afternoon, wondering what to do with himself for what was left of the day. Possibly he should look the town over, but he saw no real benefit in that. Better, he thought, to return to Aunt Lolly's, even without her sugar, get some rest and food for his deprived body.

Along the trail he found himself

thinking about Sally Shields. Who was she and where had she come from? Aunt Lolly hadn't told him except in the vaguest terms — most likely because it was none of Parthenon's business, and it wasn't, but he was naturally curious as anybody, perhaps more so because of his job.

He still had Bob Brown, or Reliance Havens (no one seemed to be sure), to worry about. A man left afoot on the desert after thinking he had stolen away with his boss's riches is bound to come back, mad. Not only had Parthenon taken his wagonload of goods away, but Barney Shivers was bound to have been alerted by now to the fact that one of his men had turned traitor. Brown would be on the run and likely out of control.

Following the sandy trail back to Lolly's little ranch, Parth began thinking about other things — like could he help his aunt bring her spread back to life? He hadn't really the amount of time to devote to such a large project.

Well, Lolly seemed happy in her small house with Sally Shields for company; perhaps she sheltered no such ambition and letting the land lie fallow and unused troubled her not at all.

At least, Parthenon thought, smiling as he rode the gray horse up a grassy bank, he had managed to solve Aunt Lolly's sugar problem for her.

His self-congratulations vanished in a puff of smoke as he crested the knoll from which Lolly's house was visible. An unseen gunman had had Parthenon in his sights and now the shot was triggered off with a following jolt of fiery pain and a rolling echo, which followed Parthenon to the ground and seemingly deeper, into the dark bowels of a thundering hell.

5

He tried to fight back at the assaulting arms, but it was useless. His blows were too feeble to beat off a 6-year-old. After a while Parthenon just lowered his defenses in surrender and let the women fuss over his wounded skull.

'I didn't know who you were,' he muttered to a woman he now recognized as his Aunt Lolly. She was making small 'tching' sounds as she worked on his scalp.

'Is that the only place they got me?' he managed to ask after Lolly took another stitch and sat back, apparently satisfied with her human embroidery.

'Wasn't that enough for you?'

Parthenon tried to nod, attempted a smile, failed at both. He was lying on his back bare-chested in a room he vaguely recognized, in Lolly's house. In a far corner of the room he could see a dim, quiet figure, hands folded before her. Sally Shields was wearing a dark blue dress with a white collar, looking as if she did not wish to be seen, was not a part of anything occurring. An invisible woman.

'How'd I get here?' Parthenon asked. Lolly was standing now, wearing a white apron with specks of blood on it. Her hair was disarranged just enough so that she felt obliged to wipe it from her forehead with the back of her hand. She studied Parthenon and finally got around to answering his question.

'You walked here — barely.'

'Walked? Where's my horse?'

'It was the horse that walked you in. You were hanging to your saddlehorn, walking beside the horse. Like a dead man walking.'

'I can imagine!' Parthenon said. 'I must have been about three miles out when I got it. There was a brilliant flash of light like sunrise in Borneo, and then everything went out. Luckily I got to my feet; luckily my horse didn't wander.'

Lolly smiled and said a little harshly, 'I don't believe you were ever in Borneo, Parth.'

'Why would I . . . ?' Then he gave it up; he had no idea why he had said that. He felt safer rolling back into his cocoon of blankets to sleep than trying to carry on a meaningful conversation, and so that was what he did.

Sounds and the scent of good cooking drew him to his feet in the early hours the following morning. He had a rough time of it trying to maintain his balance and orient himself, but he managed to walk down the hallway to Aunt Lolly's bright, clean yellow kitchen. He sagged onto a wooden chair as the two women watched him apprehensively. There was a dish with cut squares of yesterday's crumb cake on the table and so without asking, he helped himself to a square of it as Lolly poured him a cup of dark coffee and shoved a plate on the table in front of him. His manners left something to be desired and he felt a little like a schoolboy expecting to be scolded. Perhaps Lolly was feeling merciful on this morning because of his head wound; she maintained her silence as he stuffed his mouth and drank half a cup of coffee.

When his cup had been refilled and a fresh piece of cake placed on his plate, a fork provided, Lolly asked, 'What in the world did you do yesterday in Flat Rock?'

Thinking, Parthenon replied, 'Most of the day I went around doing favors for folks.'

'That would make them mad,' Lolly said with a tight smile. 'Truthfully . . . '

'That is the truth,' Parthenon said. He was starting to develop a fresh headache, and no wonder. 'I had recovered that stolen wagon from a man named Bob Brown and saw to it that the goods were delivered to the people they had been intended for.'

'Then it must have been this Bob

Brown who shot you, wouldn't you say?'

'He'd be my first guess. I was told that his real name might be Reliance Havens — does that name mean anything to you?'

'No, it doesn't.'

'Well, you probably would not have moved in the same circles. I just asked because he seems to have been from Flat Rock. Maybe not.'

'Well,' Lolly said, rising from the table, 'all I can tell you is that he was not one of our Sunday tea group. But I'm certain I never heard of him before.'

As they spoke, Parthenon had noticed that Sally Shields stood nervously near the back door as she had on his last visit, seeming ready to bolt at any unwelcome attention. Parthenon had glanced at the withdrawn woman from time to time and felt only pity.

That, and more than a little curiosity. When the name Reliance

Havens was mentioned, Sally blanched, closed her eyes tightly for a moment and then pressed her hands more tightly together. She knew the name; Parth was sure of that. He found himself unable to ask her directly. She was so shy as to seem broken — a young bird who has failed in her first attempt at taking wing and crashed to the ground to remain there, fearful eyes watching, waiting for destruction, unable to flee.

'Now that you've had your dessert,' Lolly was saying, 'how about an egg or two to cap off your meal?'

'No thanks. If no one minds, though, I think I'd like to be outside for a while, breathe some fresh air, see if it helps or hinders. Maybe I'll go over and see to my horse.' Parthenon got to his feet, the wooden chair legs scraping on the floor.

'So's it don't get lonely?' Lolly, a woman who had not been around horses much asked, as if it didn't happen. All animals can feel sadly neglected if their owner is absent for too long, horses definitely included.

'Let me look at that head wound before you go,' Lolly said. 'Just sit back down. That was a near thing,' she added. 'If your head had been turned an inch or two — '

'I know,' Parthenon replied. Before he could be seated again, Sally had slipped from the room. Maybe the talk of death had made up her mind to disappear into some dark, secret place.

'The girl seems to be hurt more than me,' Parthenon said as Lolly unwrapped the bandaging on his head to examine the wound.

'Sally? She's not hurting!' Lolly said with a light laugh.

'Yes, she is, and you know it. What happened to her, Lolly?'

'Something everyone knows but no one is supposed to talk about,' Lolly answered, fingering her recent stitch work on Parthenon's head as she spoke. 'I think I'll dab some more carbolic on this, just in case.'

She turned away to fetch the needed

implements. Parthenon heard a steel bowl clatter in the sink, and the sound of cupboard doors opening and closing as Lolly searched for her weapons of torture. 'I am a member of the family,' Parthenon reminded his aunt, 'and a lawman.'

'Not *her* family, and talking to the law hasn't gotten us very far up to now.'

The bowl was placed on the table and some of the evil-smelling carbolic acid, slightly diluted, splashed into it. 'Hold on to your suspenders,' Lolly said, 'here we go again,' and she began swabbing the carbolic over his scalp as she softly whistled an almost cheerful tune.

'How's that feel?' Lolly asked.

'Just like you think it does,' Parth replied, his eyes squinted tightly shut as much as from the burning sting as to keep the terrible liquid from dripping into his eyes.

'It's supposed to feel like that if it's doing any good,' Lolly said. 'Like what they say about medicine — if it doesn't taste awful, it can't help you.' She continued as if it were part of the same line of conversation. 'Now Sally is Barney Shivers's daughter . . . '

'She's what!' Parthenon shouted, twisting in his chair enough to cause Lolly to miss her target. Carbolic filled his ear.

'Shush! Sit still. Everyone knows that; you being from the far reaches wouldn't. That is,' Lolly went on with a sigh, 'his wife was her mother. Monica Shields was her name. Sally's his stepdaughter,' she said, explaining her different name.

'Being from the far reaches,' Parthenon said as Lolly put the pan down in the sink with a clatter, 'I know nothing about any of this — what happened to Sally's mother?'

'Why, that's no mystery, of course. Barney Shivers paid someone to have Monica killed.'

'But why? For another woman, I suppose.'

'That's right,' Lolly said. 'Of course

she's gone now too.' Lolly was unwrapping a roll of fresh bandaging.

'But if everyone knows — '

'Well, everyone knows. But it wouldn't stand up in court, Parth. Barney Shivers was off at Placer's Dance Hall all that night. Playing cards with friends who would vouch for that. When he got home a little after midnight, he claims he saw a light on in the upstairs window and then the shadowy figure of a man breaking from the house toward his horse. Barney discovered his wife dead on the floor.'

'Nobody ever found the supposed killer, then?'

'Marshal Keyser, he got a posse up and tracked the man the next morning for as far as they could follow the tracks, but they lost him.'

'And nobody had any idea of who it might have been — if there even was such a man?'

'Everybody had an idea,' Lolly said. 'Everyone knew who it was, everyone but the marshal, who, if he knew, was content to pretend he didn't.'

'Who, then, Aunt Lolly? Who killed Sally's mother?'

'Why — everyone knows! It was Golden Loggins who done it.'

Parthenon frowned. 'Golden Loggins — that young man who's running another freight line out of Flat Rock?'

'Yes,' Lolly said, tightening a knot in the bandage. 'Now you can quit wondering how Barney Shivers tolerates him when he's broken the back of every other small freighter in the country.'

'That stinks,' Parthenon said.

Lolly, misunderstanding, told him, 'The fresh air will clear most of that away when you step outside.'

When he was outside on the porch, a fresh breeze blowing, the stink lingered. Not of the carbolic, but of the situation in which Parthenon now found himself, if all was as Lolly Amos believed. Would she lie? No, but she might have gotten some of the local gossip mixed up with the facts.

Parthenon had learned to hold in doubt any statement which began with 'everyone knows'. If Lolly seemed sure of her facts, still she couldn't have known. There just wasn't enough evidence to convict either man of participation in the murder of Barney Shivers's wife, which was probably the reason local folks felt that they were not getting the action they demanded from Marshal Keyser. Keyser knew that he could not get a conviction on this sort of hearsay evidence. A judge would throw it out of court before the jury had the time to get settled in their seats.

It was not only a matter of trying to convict prominent local men, but of not even having a single witness to the crime . . . or was there one?

Was that Sally Shields's secret, the reason behind the fear in her eyes: the knowledge that her mother had been killed and if she dared speak up, she could be next?

Parthenon wished that he could talk to the girl, but knew she would not allow it. Who else was there to talk to? Well, the man named as the killer, Golden Loggins. In fact Loggins had earlier asked him to come by his house that evening. Maybe the freighter knew something about this. He certainly must have been miffed if he had been labeled the killer in the death of Monica Shivers. And who had named him as such?

Parthenon had reached the barn and he busied himself currying the gray horse. He realized that an investigation into the murder of Sally Shields's mother was far afield from his looking into the land piracy in the area, but he felt an obligation to at least take a deeper look at the case.

Not least of all because two of the main players in the murder were Golden Loggins and Barney Shivers himself, the owners of the two freight lines run out of Flat Rock.

When Parthenon had taken on the task of finding the cargo thieves, it had been his own dubious decision, not that of his boss, Gabe Lindquist. There had been no order of business, no boundaries set for the job, which probably had seemed to Lindquist to be an impossible one Parthenon was only taking on to get out of the office for a while. Nevertheless it was Parthenon's bronco and it was his to throw and brand — if he could.

As Lolly fussed with her kitchen, readying the evening meal, Parthenon annoyed her with a few more questions.

'Why is Golden Loggins the main suspect? You never did tell me.'

'Did I say he was a suspect?' Lolly said rather sternly, turning to stand before Parth with her arms crossed over her apron, one of her hands holding a wooden cooking spoon. 'I did not — I said that he was the one who had done the murder!'

'But, if he wasn't seen by someone . . . '

Lolly turned away again as he spoke. 'He was seen, Parthenon, and not only after the event but during it.' Her

83

gesture was a very slight one, but Lolly inclined her head in the direction of the hallway where Parthenon had last seen Sally Shields.

'Then why . . . ?'

'Parthenon,' Lolly snapped, 'leave me alone! You're as much trouble as you were when you were five years old hanging around bothering me — you've made me salt the potatoes twice!'

He was holding up Lolly's production and it seemed he was not going to get much new, usable information anyway. Lolly had apparently been Sally's confidante, but it seemed she had been sworn to secrecy concerning some points in the girl's revelations. Maybe Sally had wished it so to try to protect Lolly as well.

'I won't be here for dinner, Aunt Lolly,' Parthenon said, rising from the table. 'I have some more work to do. I'm going to ride over to Golden Loggins's place. He'll be able to tell me more about Barney Shivers and his methods of work than anyone else. If he will. He seemed willing to talk earlier.'

'Probably he just wants to find out about Sally,' Lolly said as Parth hesitated in the doorway, his hat in hand.

'Because of the murder, you mean?'

'Among other things,' Lolly said. 'Those two were a little more tangled up in matters than you know. Sally Shields was set to marry Golden Loggins at one time.'

That left Parthenon with a bushel of new questions, but he could tell that Lolly was not going to answer any of them. Positioning his hat, he walked out into the wind-swept yard, shoulders hunched, to return to the barn where he meant to saddle his gray and make his way to the house of the man who now seemed to be at the heart of matters — Golden Loggins.

6

There were meadowlarks in the tall grass and a light breeze shifting the high reaches of the cottonwood trees when he again rode over the knoll where he had been ambushed the night before. The memory of the attack seemed to cause his injured skull to throb more violently with pain. He thought perhaps he should try to find a doctor in Flat Rock if they had one, but probably Lolly had already done as much as anyone could.

That crease along his scalp had been a near thing. Lolly had been right about that. A slight difference in the way he had been carrying his head had meant the difference between life and death. The way he had folded up and fallen from his pony may have indicated to the would-be killer that he had done his job. Parthenon was only glad that the man had not come nearer to finish his work. Out cold at the time, Parthenon would have been helpless to resist a killing shot.

Now as he crested the hill, looking down again on the town of Flat Rock, he let his breath out, not even realizing that he had been holding it in. There had been some shadowy fear that the rifleman would try again if he passed the same way, but now, approaching the town, that unfounded uneasiness passed.

And so it was as he dipped down into the sandy wash fronting the slowly running silver creek that he was completely unprepared for the rider with the unsheathed rifle who emerged from among the trees and called out a warning.

'Draw that pony up or I'll shoot you where you are!'

Parthenon was in no position to ask questions and so he drew in the gray and waited, hands hanging loosely.

Finally, as the horseman approached

and could be spoken to without yelling, Parth asked,

'Why are you stopping me? You don't know me and I've no money in my poke.'

'I'm not after money, and I don't need to know who you are — you've got that look about you. Trying to find some work in Flat Rock, are you?'

'I've got business there,' Parthenon replied.

'Who with?' the rider, who was now nearly within reach, sitting a small pinto pony asked.

She might have been trying to disguise it, but it was perfectly obvious that she was a young woman by the way her dark hair was fashioned under the gray flop hat she wore and the too-womanly way she filled her gray work shirt and blue jeans. That did not relieve Parthenon's mind much. A woman with a rifle was at least as dangerous as a man. Maybe more so. They got skittish quicker and were more likely to pull the trigger if they felt threatened.

'I am going to see a man named Golden Loggins, if I can find him,' Parth answered. 'And then to visit another called Barney Shivers.'

'That's what I thought,' the girl said in a triumphant voice. 'I could tell by your rough looks that you were that sort of man. Take my advice, stranger,' she said, leaning closer, 'there is no work for you or any of your kind in Flat Rock — those days are over.'

'You seem to have me wrong,' Parthenon said, tilting his hat back, which revealed his cap of bandaging.

'You've been shot,' the small young woman exclaimed with an audible gasp.

'I have — was that some of your work?'

'I wouldn't, I couldn't — '

'You're the only one I've met with killing intentions out here,' Parthenon said.

'Oh, I wasn't . . . ' she said with a small squeak in her voice.

'And the Territory of Arizona doesn't take kindly to having their rangers shot down. They'd come after you, you know. And there's no chance of running and hiding once they do.'

Parthenon had swung around slightly in the saddle so that the sunlight now mirrored brightly off his Captain's badge. She lowered her rifle; her eyes grew astonished. 'I didn't know,' she said. 'I thought — '

'That I was just a wandering man looking for work you could feel free to shoot down along the trail?'

'No. It's not that,' she said with frustration. The wind lifted the front of her hat brim and she clamped a hand over it. 'If I could explain — '

'I would have listened if you had not come across my trail armed to kill. I still might — put that Winchester away where it belongs!' Parthenon said with force. He had been shot once in this country and did not wish to repeat the event. Not even accidentally at the hands of this wild young woman. She dutifully slipped the rifle back into its scabbard.

Parthenon told her, 'I talk better standing on the ground. That way I don't have to worry about you suddenly slapping spurs to that pinto and taking off on me.'

'All right,' she replied. 'Whatever you say, mister.'

She looked like she had lost the urge to talk, but she swung down from the little pinto and walked around the gray's flanks to stand facing Parthenon. A little of her belligerence returned to her dark eyes as Parth dismounted.

Parthenon, leading his horse, moved to the welcome shade of a white oak tree. He stood for a moment, looking from the knoll to the town below. 'All right,' he said sharply, 'why don't you tell me what you're doing out here? It's obvious you didn't come out riding for your health. In fact you may have a sort of death wish, bracing men you don't know with that rifle of yours.'

Parthenon had sagged to the base of

the oak, and was now seated on the ground, knees drawn up. He tipped the hat back from his bandaged head. At a motion of invitation, the girl found a shaded seat not far from his. She began energetically shredding a fallen oak leaf.

'Oh, I don't know what's gotten into me,' she said, 'I was never this way before.'

'Before what?' Parthenon prompted.

'Well, you try it!' she said with sudden vehemence. She removed her hat and sailed it away a few yards so that her dark hair tumbled free. 'Having the only man you ever loved sent to kill a woman you had known as your mother, finding out that your own father had paid him to do the job. Then discovering, as much as you had always tried not to believe it, that both of them were among the biggest crooks in Arizona!'

'I see,' Parthenon muttered. Essentially, these were the facts that Parthenon himself had gathered concerning the events around Flat Rock.

But where did this girl fit in? Who was she? She had spoken as if she must be Sally Shields's sister, stepsister, something like that. How many children and how many wives had Barney Shivers had? Did he think of all of them as disposable?

'You're speaking, of course, of Golden Loggins and Barney Shivers,' Parthenon tried for clarification. The girl looked for a moment as if she couldn't catch her breath.

'You're the law; I'm not sure I should be talking to you.'

'Then don't,' Parthenon said as if it made no difference to him. In fact it did not. He leaned back on one elbow as the breeze shifted the shade of the oak this way and that. The girl was busy shredding another broad leaf.

'What's your name?' Parthenon demanded abruptly.

She began to tremble. 'Why, what difference does it make to you?'

'Well,' he told the startled girl, 'I've got a little book I carry with the names of those who have tried to kill me so that I know who to come looking for later.'

'I didn't try to kill you,' she said defensively.

'You offered to,' Parthenon replied coldly. 'Let me ask you again — what's your name?'

She looked down at the earth, wagging her head stubbornly.

'I see, you're one of those who only does her talking when she has a gun in her hand.' He waited. She blurted out:

'Margaret Havens is my name! Don't call me 'Maggie', I don't like it.'

'I wasn't planning on it,' Parth answered. *Havens* she had said — as in Reliance Havens? Parthenon's mind was whirling, finding no pattern on which to settle itself. He decided to slow things down a little.

'Why don't you tell me about it all, Margaret? I need to understand what's happening around Flat Rock.'

'Why?' she asked.

'So I can help clean things up.'

'I don't see what you could . . . ' a sigh broke her words off and she leaned back, propped up on both elbows. She looked into the distance, the wind ruffling her dark hair. She brushed a strand or two from her eyes. Then she returned her attention to Parthenon. 'I don't know why you need to know this or why I'm telling you,' she said, 'but this is what happened . . . '

★   ★   ★

There were only two light taps on the front door of the Shivers's house, but it was enough to awaken the two young half-sisters who had been sleeping restlessly in adjoining upstairs rooms on the hot August evening. Both heard Monica Shivers's light footsteps as she crossed the downstairs living room, expecting her husband, Barney, home from his night's gambling and carousing at Placer's Dance Hall in Flat Rock.

It was an unusual, but hardly unique occurrence for Barney, who Monica knew liked his whiskey and loved his women — no one had ever accused Barney Shivers of being a one-woman man.

The downstairs door, instead of being filled by a reeling Shivers, was slammed open by two men wearing dark bandannas as masks. Sally Shields had been the first out of her upstairs room, and by the dim light of the homecoming lantern in the room below, she saw the men burst in, grab Monica and throw her roughly aside.

'Where is he?' one of the masked men growled, but before Monica, struggling to her feet, could answer, she was thrown aside again. Sally had cried out at this point, and one of the men briefly glanced upward to the head of the stairs.

Margaret, also in her nightgown, had reached Sally and placed her hand over her mouth.

'Be quiet,' Margaret had warned in a hiss, 'can't you see those men are in a killing mood?'

Sally had struggled in Margaret's arms, but gave it up as one of the men again approached her mother. His hat had been knocked off and they could see a shock of blond hair — it was Golden Loggins, both thought. He stood over Monica for long seconds, her eyes watching him with anguished fear. The man lowered the hammer on his Colt without discharging a shot and turned away.

'Can't do it?' the second, indistinguishable man asked. And stepping forward he executed the poor sheltering woman on the floor. Gunsmoke rose and clotted the air of the room.

'You didn't have to do that,' the hatless man said.

'Didn't I? What else did we come here for?'

Sally Shields had passed out in Margaret's arms and so she never saw the finish to matters. The tall blond man bent to snatch his hat from the varnished floor. The other one growled, 'Now the girls.'

'No you don't,' the tall man had warned his accomplice. 'That was never a part of the arrangement — or I wouldn't have come at all.'

'They're witnesses,' the shorter man argued.

'In this light with us wearing masks, what could they have seen? Light out for town; I'll lead any posse into the badlands. We've got to be out of here before he gets home.'

There were a few more muttered, unintelligible words and then the men left the house, riding in opposite directions, leaving the small, sad physical remains of Monica Shivers puddled against the floor.

★   ★   ★

'Is that it?' Parthenon Downs asked as the small dark-eyed girl sat shivering in the shade of the old oaks.

'It's all I know. What else do you want me to tell you?'

'I don't know,' Parthenon said. What

else was there that he needed to know? Except for the fact that it was second-hand knowledge passed on to him by a girl who had to have been half-hysterical at the time, it seemed obvious that Golden Loggins and the other man were the ones who had broken into the Shivers's house, come with instructions to deliberately kill Monica.

His first question was, 'It was dark, and they were wearing masks. What makes you so sure it was Golden Loggins that you saw from upstairs?'

'I know Golden, the way he walks. It was him; I saw that beautiful yellow hair of his.'

'I doubt he's the only man around Flat Rock with yellow hair,' Parthenon pointed out. 'Did his accomplice call him by name, or did you just make the assumption because it happened in your house?'

'Oh, I don't know,' Margaret said, looking flustered now. 'Who else could have been hired to do the job?'

'You said that the men discussed the necessity of leaving before he got home. Are you even sure Barney Shivers had hired the job done?'

'I know Barney Shivers!' Margaret insisted. 'Much better than you do. He had my own mother killed when he decided he wanted Monica Shields.'

'And you're sure of that, are you? Was he ever tried for your mother's murder?'

'People don't arrest Barney Shivers in this part of the country — not for anything!'

The girl seemed certain enough in her own mind, but she had offered no compelling evidence. Possibly she hated Barney Shivers enough to believe everything was his fault. Parthenon didn't know. It was a complex business.

'If you knew that one of the men was Golden Loggins, why didn't you speak up when the marshal was asking questions?'

'Tell Sam Keyser? As if that would do

any good. He's in with that whole bunch!' She clamped her jaw shut and refused to meet his eyes.

To Parthenon it seemed that there might be more to this. 'Did you love Golden Loggins? Is that why you kept quiet?'

'Of course I did,' Margaret said, still without raising her eyes. 'He used to come out to the house to talk to Barney and to see me — quite often. I didn't realize it at first, but it became quite obvious that he was seeing me only to be close to Sally.'

'You can't be sure of that.'

'I am!' she snapped.

'All right,' Parthenon said, trying to soothe her. 'If so, then why would Golden agree to kill Sally's mother?'

'She wasn't to know. It was cooked up between Golden and Barney. Barney had found himself a new honey — I've seen her a few times. Her name is Lou Sessions. She worked at the Placer's Dance Hall, as they call the place,' Margaret added disparagingly.

101

'She worked for Dwight Charles, then?'

'You've met him? You do get around, don't you? Yes, Charles was her boss.'

'So Shivers wanted to get rid of Monica, you say. That takes me back to wondering why Golden Loggins would agree to take part in such a plan.'

'Why? He wanted to be as rich as Barney Shivers, and he knew he could not fight Barney and win. He needed Shivers's favor to stay in business. Besides,' she said, now lifting her eyes to meet his, 'Barney had agreed to let him have Sally as part of his pay.'

Looking to the sky, Parthenon said, 'I see.' He rose, dusted his jeans with his hands and told her, 'I believe I've heard everything you have to say. Or will say.'

'But you don't believe me,' Margaret said, also rising. She stood shaking a little. She looked around for her hat. Parthenon finally answered:

'I believe you've told me everything you saw, everything you believe to be true. Now it's time to talk to a man who knows precisely what happened.'

'Golden Loggins!'

'That's right. I already told you that's where I was headed.' He walked toward his horse. The girl stood wistfully by as if wishing she could ride to Loggins's house with him. She still hadn't made up her mind whether she loved the man or hated him, it seemed.

'I'll leave you out here to do your mischief, Miss Havens. Be careful you don't level that rifle at some man who's not in a talking mood. It's always a little embarrassing to be shot, especially when it's your own fault.'

She sputtered some sort of answer. But there were no words from her lips. Her own mind was too tangled up with angry emotions for her to sort them logically. Parthenon turned the gray's head and started down the long slope through the oak trees toward the not-so-sleepy town of Flat Rock.

As Loggins had told him, everyone in town knew where he lived. Asking for instructions only twice along his way,

103

he came upon a neat little white-frame house, sitting among mature oak trees. Well, of course Golden Loggins would have dressed lumber and fresh paint for his own home. He had easy access to these relatively rare materials.

It was a comfortable-looking place with a single stone chimney at the center. Was this home built for Sally Shields? A mangy old white dog came forward on arthritis-crippled legs, looking up at Parthenon hopefully as it wagged its broom tail. The dog was not there for security, that was for sure. Besides, Parthenon knew, the house was well secured. Outlaw captains do not like surprise visits, and their property was always well guarded. He didn't need to see the man with the rifle in the window to see that Golden Loggins's fortress was no different.

7

Parthenon had not seen Golden riding a horse that day, but there was a tall strapping black at the white-painted iron hitch rail that could have belonged to the desert prince. Nearby in the shadow of an oak a two-horse surrey sat, the two bay horses dozing in the mottled sunlight. A man dressed all in black stood nearby, leaning casually against an oak tree. There was a dangerous look about him.

Who could that buggy belong to? The little vehicle suggested wealth and someone who liked his comfort. Could it be that the top dog, Barney Shivers himself was visiting Golden Loggins at the same time as Parthenon?

Many things could be, Parthenon reminded himself. The way you found out the answers was to approach the questions directly, not by beating around in conjecture. He stepped up onto the porch of the white house and knocked twice on the heavy, varnished door.

When the door swung open it was Bob Brown whose face Parthenon saw. 'You don't want to come in here,' Brown said in a threatening voice.

'But I do,' Parthenon answered. Brown still had the hard look in his eyes that he had worn at Vulture Hole. He was still unshaven, wearing what looked to be the same clothes. Parthenon wondered how the man's boots were holding up — he had had a long walk to Flat Rock. A memory of every mile of it was reflected in Brown's tight expression.

'I said you weren't welcome here,' Brown said, holding his rifle a little more tightly now.

'I was invited, Havens,' Parthenon said, shouldering his way into the wide living room heedless of Bob Brown's rifle and objections.

'What did you call me?' Bob Brown said, facing Parthenon with his Winchester clenched in both hands. The glare in his eyes was such as Parthenon might have caused if he had cursed the man.

'Havens. Isn't that your name? By the way, I met your daughter just now.' Parthenon was playing it recklessly, but he was feeling reckless, and was in no mood to be turned away by such as Bob Brown.

'You couldn't've met my daughter,' Brown said.

'I did, but that has nothing to do with why I'm here. Where is he?'

'Who d'ya mean?'

'Why Golden Loggins, of course. Who else could have invited me out here?'

'Golden wouldn't have invited no lawman to his house,' Brown said with certainty.

'You're wrong; he did. Now where is he?'

'I don't know if what you say is true.

How do I know he asked you to his house?'

'You don't,' Parthenon replied. 'So why don't you just go along and ask him?'

'I will,' Brown said with a flare-up of anger. He reminded Parthenon, 'I haven't forgotten about what you did to me out at Vulture Hole.'

'I didn't expect you to,' Parth told him. 'I was hoping, however, that it might have taught you a lesson.'

'I don't need no lessons from the likes of you,' Brown snarled. He still had not made a move toward the interior of the house. He stood hunched forward, shaking slightly with anger.

'Yes, you do. Some time when I have a lot of time to explain it to you, I will.'

'Why, you're nothin' but a dog wearing a ranger's star,' Brown said almost in a pant. His face and voice were those of a man who truly hated. For a moment Parthenon thought that Brown was going to shoulder his rifle, but just then Golden Loggins entered the room.

'What are you doing, Bob?' Golden asked sharply. 'When I tell a man to stand watch, this is not what I have I mind!'

Smoothly he turned his almost boyish eyes on Parthenon and said, 'I see you managed to find me. Welcome to my house, Downs.'

Bob Brown walked away grumbling. Parthenon thought he had just been given an indication of Golden Loggins's actual nature: curt, sharp with those he believed to be his inferiors; smooth and civilized with those he thought he would be forced to deal with.

'Is Barney Shivers here?' Parthenon asked. He was not a spy of any sort; why not come out and ask exactly what he wished to know.

'He was for a few minutes. He's just gone.'

'Without his buggy and his body-guard?' Parthenon asked.

A deep, commanding voice sounded

from the door-way where Golden Loggins had entered the room.

'Oh, for God's sake, Golden! There's no need to play games with the ranger. I'm here,' the bulky, square man who had to be Barney Shivers boomed. 'Golden and I had some business to discuss. Tell me, Ranger, what brings you here?'

'You couldn't guess?' Parthenon asked, seating himself on a black leather sofa without having been invited to. 'I'm down here from Tucson investigating a major hijacking ring. There's a lot more under that umbrella term — robbery, wrongful possession of stolen goods, assault and battery on wagon drivers — '

'No murders?' Shivers asked with a sneer.

'Not that have come up yet. We do have an attempted murder of a state officer, though.'

'Against you?' Golden Loggins asked, attempting to look shocked and puzzled at once.

Maybe he was. That or he was a good actor. Parthenon shifted on the sofa, recrossing his legs. His eyes were steely now as they moved from Loggins to Barney Shivers.

'Against me,' Parth told them. He touched his bandaged head. 'Those are the charges relating to these wagon hijackings, but there are other charges against each of you that will have to be resolved.'

'Charges?' Golden repeated, still with a blank expression.

'What are you up to, Ranger? Other matters unrelated to the supposed hijackings can't concern you,' Shivers said with stolid resistance in his voice.

'Oh, they can, sir. Arizona is not selective about investigating crimes. If a ranger comes across one he is expected to look into it.'

'What sorts of crimes are you referring to now?' Golden asked, his eyes narrowed.

'Capital murder and murder for hire come to mind,' Parthenon told them.

His eyes remained hard. Golden twitched a bit, feeling he knew what was coming. Barney Shivers laughed and bellowed at once.

'What are you talking about, Ranger, or do you even know?' the fat merchant demanded.

'Oh, I know,' Parthenon said, still not rising from the comfortable sofa, 'and you do too.'

'Do I?' Shivers was challenging, sure of his own power. Golden Loggins looked less confident. Parthenon decided to try shaking the big man up.

'What happened to your first wife, Shivers? What became of Margaret Havens' mother?'

Shivers's face tightened with anger or simple frustration. 'She died of cholera, and that was a long time ago, Ranger . . . if it's any of your business.'

'I don't know if it is or not — yet. And your next wife, Shivers? What happened to Sally Shields's mother, Monica?'

Shivers blanched; his eyes seemed to

come loose in their sockets for a second, then focused on Parthenon with intense hate. 'Is that what you're fishing for?' Barney Shivers asked in his customary bellow. 'She was murdered recently, but not at my hand, and you damned well know it! The law knows it; all of the people in the vicinity of Flat Rock know it!'

'Does Golden Loggins here know it?' Parthenon prodded. The younger, yellow-haired man who had not expected the conversation to veer his way, paled as much as Barney Shivers had. They were both obviously having an unhappy evening, and Parthenon was the one to blame.

'I'll be going,' Parth said, judging the time was right for his departure. 'I'll be seeing you,' he said to Golden. 'I may return; as long as these wagons keep coming up missing, it'll keep me around for quite some time — until I've broken the back of these land pirates.' He tipped his hat to Golden, stared for a moment more at Barney Shivers, then nodded and stepped out onto the porch of the house.

Had he given too much of his game away? Maybe, but it had to be done, and he had come up with no other way to do it than to let the hijackers know that he was on to them.

Proving any of it was a different matter. In the murder of the Shields woman he had two witnesses but both were unreliable. The girls were unlikely to convince a jury of what they had seen. Sally Shields might not be willing to testify at all. Margaret was a quick-tempered girl, her mood changing rapidly. She was as likely to decide that she was in love with Golden again and be unwilling to come forward in court.

As to the desert piracy, Parthenon had not a single man who would give evidence. Reliance Havens had been caught with a wagonload of stolen goods, but either Golden Loggins or Barney Shivers was likely to say he was working for them, that he had recovered the wagon, that an over-eager Arizona ranger, looking to make a name for himself had stolen it back from Reliance.

No, Parthenon admitted to himself, he had hardly enough on any of these men to take to court and expect the evidence to stand up.

He had to attack the problem from a different angle. It seemed that the best way was to discover how the entire scheme worked. Where, for example, were the hijacked wagons kept before their 'recovery' by Loggins and Shivers? Where did the pirate crews live? How did they know which of the short-line haulers would be carrying a load worth taking?

It was a large problem with many questions, and at that moment Parth doubted he could solve it on his own. Maybe he should have tried harder to get Gabriel Lindquist to allow him to recruit a few more rangers from out of their ranks. Men to watch the railroad terminus, to follow rich wagonloads, men to get themselves hired on to the outlaws' ranks.

Parthenon knew that Lindquist would never have allowed that. The ranger ranks were already spread thin, and Parth had no particular target in mind that the rangers could attack. Nothing but suspicions, nothing but what amounted to spy work to offer, which was never the particular skill of the bunches of hard-riding, quick-shooting men they had working for them.

No, Parth found himself thinking as he rode from Golden Loggins's yard, his first idea had been the best, and the one with the greater likelihood of success. He knew now who the organizers of the pirates were; the thing to do was cut the head off the snake.

As he left the area of the white house he saw that Barney Shivers had gone, taking his black-clad bodyguard with him. Probably he was heading home to plan his future operations — and likely to figure what to do about Parthenon

Downs, who had buzzed in to Flat Rock like an annoying insect who refused to leave. Shivers could not let his entire, quite profitable enterprise be upset by one insignificant man just because he happened to be wearing a badge.

Reliance Havens stood near the barn in the strip of shadow its roof cast, still glaring, still gripping his Winchester in both hands, no doubt wishing he could use it on Parthenon. Probably his wages had been docked for failing to bring the stolen wagon in, for letting Parthenon trick him out of possession. It seemed that Havens worked for Golden and not for Barney Shivers. Could he, then, have been the other masked man who had come to kill Monica Shivers? Parthenon remembered that according to Margaret, that man had been willing to kill the daughters to cover their tracks, that Golden Loggins was the one to talk him out of those murders.

Could Reliance Havens be a man who was so cold that he would kill his own daughter minutes after shooting her mother to death? The idea was immediately dismissed from his mind, even though from his years in the company of criminals, he knew there were indeed some men who would kill their own mother for a few dollars.

He thought that the girls had both been wrong in their identifications, or lied about them.

As he had told Margaret, there were plenty of men with yellow hair around. Margaret had said she knew it was Golden by the way he moved, walked, held himself; shouldn't that have applied even more strongly in the case of Reliance Havens, if he was one of the killers?

Surely she knew the physical attributes of her own father no matter how long he had been away. Away where? And why? If it was Shivers who had taken his wife from him, why would Reliance work for the man, do his bidding?

As he had been considering earlier,

the rangers were competent fighting men, but hardly cut out to do detective work. Parthenon counted himself among the former. This situation had too many threads his mind could not follow. He returned to his first thought — sever the two-headed snake from its body, but how, without doing murder himself?

He had one more thought that seemed outrageous on its surface, but possibly could cut through the snarled knot. He pondered that idea as he crested the low, oak-studded hill that he had crossed before . . .

He was shot from his saddle by a hidden rifleman. The roar of the Winchester near at hand was explosive, the sharp jolt of a heavy lead slug stunning as it passed through his body and sent Parthenon sprawling to the earth, his gray horse dancing away, reins trailing. For the moment his entire body felt numbed and his vision was blurred. He tried to crawl, to roll away from where he lay, but his limbs refused to cooperate. He was forced to simply lie there, staring up at the brightly lit tips of the trees, the pale, hot sky beyond. He could not even roll his head to look in the direction of the stealthy figure approaching from across the clearing. He could not make the person out clearly, but he saw the rifle in his hands, the glint of sunlight on its long barrel.

'Reliance?' he managed to mutter, his words sounding as if his mouth was filled with pebbles.

'No. It's me,' a quiet voice answered, and Parthenon could now make out the features of Margaret Havens.

'I guess I shouldn't have given you a second chance,' Parthenon said, his voice a little more distinct now, but sounding distant in his ears, as if he were speaking from miles away.

'Oh, shut up,' Margaret said, kneeling beside him. As she did she placed her rifle aside. 'I didn't shoot you — I told you that I'm not that kind.'

'Then you must have seen who did

it.' Parthenon said. The girl lifted his head and offered him a trickle of water from her canteen. He became aware that his hand was gripping her wrist too tightly, and let it fall away. 'Your father? Did he follow me up here?'

'No, it wasn't Reliance.'

'But you know who did it?' Parthenon asked. She nodded her head.

'I saw him. He was coming over to finish the job when I rode up and he took to his heels when he saw me. It was Quirt Gaffey.' Parthenon's face must have been blank. She went on to explain, 'You'll usually find him around wherever you find Barney Shivers.'

'Quirt . . . ?'

'Gaffey. If you were down at Golden's house you must have seen him. He's most always dressed in black.'

Of course — the bodyguard Parthenon had seen keeping watch over Barney Shiver's rig while his boss went into the house. Margaret said in a voice which trembled a little:

121

'You're leaking a lot of blood. I'll do what I can to bind up your chest, but you're going to need help. Where were you going when I found you? I'll get you there.'

'I was headed for Placer's Dance Hall.'

'Oh, I see,' Margaret's eyes narrowed. He remembered she had a low opinion of the place.

'It's nothing you might think. I had an idea that might help my investigation.' He thought, also, of Dwight Charles, the owner, telling him that he was welcome at his place any time. That and he had been offered a room at the hotel, at no cost, by the Dutchman and his wife. Well he would be calling in those markers much sooner than he had expected. He hoped honestly that one good turn did deserve another in Flat Rock.

In half an hour they were mounted and on their way toward the small desert town. He doubted that the hasty bandaging Margaret had done was doing much good, but she had made the offer and it was a welcome one. Almost as welcome as the assist she gave him onto the gray's back without which Parthenon could not have reached leather without a step ladder.

'Are you sure you want to go back to Flat Rock?' Margaret asked as they began winding their way down the hills through the oaks.

'I think I have to,' Parthenon said.

'Why not go to your aunt's place? You were staying there, weren't you? You've got a girl at home to think of,' Margaret said, looking away into the distance.

'Do you mean Sally?' Parthenon tried to avoid a laugh. 'I haven't spoken one word to her. She wouldn't answer if I did. And I did not come to Flat Rock looking for a girl.'

'Where, then, are we going?'

'To Placer's, as I told you, Margaret.'

'To Placer's, but you're not looking for a girl.'

'No, not of that kind . . . not of any kind.'

'All right,' Margaret agreed without cheer. 'But, Ranger, you sure do know all of the right places to look for trouble.'

8

Flat Rock when they reached it was, to Parthenon's eyes, only a blur of white sand, ferociously blue skies and small drops of blood. Margaret halted their ponies in a narrow alley which was unfamiliar to Parthenon.

Looking at him clinically, she asked, 'Are you sure you want to go to Placer's just now? It's a rough place, you know, and most of its crowd are the kind of men who would enjoy seeing a ranger in the shape you're in. Besides, what good could you possibly do yourself right now?'

'You're right, I suppose,' Parthenon answered. The world was beginning to swim crazily in his vision. 'Better take me to the Dutchman's hotel, then find me some sort of doctor.'

'That's better thinking,' Margaret agreed. 'You aren't in shape to fight off a fly. You can find your woman later.'

She was right, of course. He had to get some rest and some medical attention now. There was always time to find Lou Sessions later — if she lived that long. It was said that she broke it off with Barney Shivers as he was expecting her to marry him. What would that mean for her? Shivers had exhibited only extreme decisions in his attitude toward women. He married them in haste, then disposed of them in an equally violent manner.

Did Lou Sessions have a child? Both of the last two Parthenon was aware of had a young daughter when they went to live with Shivers. It did not matter to Parthenon what the man's motives were.

It was his actions that must be halted.

Margaret, who knew her way around town, led them up an anonymous alley to the rear of the Dutchman's hotel. His round little wife was on the back porch, shaking out a dust mop. The woman lifted her eyes, shielded them from the sunlight with her hand, and seemed to gasp silently.

'Well, here we are,' Margaret said as the Dutch wife darted back inside the hotel. 'What's it like in one of these places? I've never been to a hotel myself.'

'They're all right, except it's kind of living like there's no such things as outdoors. At least I'll have a new mattress,' Parthenon said with effortful amusement. He was grimacing in pain when he said this last and Margaret saw she would soon have to get him from his horse or he would topple from it.

Fortunately, the Dutchman himself emerged onto the back porch just then, his wife at his shoulder. The man had never offered his name and Parthenon had no need to know it. He hadn't honestly expected to ever see the Dutchman again, certainly not this soon. The hotel owner came forward and Parthenon slipped from the saddle into his powerful arms and was lowered to the earth.

'I don't think he can walk,' Margaret said.

'Don't worry! I can carry. I will take care of him.'

The terrific sunlight was suddenly blotted out by a roof and Parthenon, feeling like a fool, was carried into the building by the Dutchman. It was not the first time such a thing had happened to Parth, but he hoped it would be the last. He found himself thinking back to Lindquist's last interview with him, the one about men getting a little too old and slow for this job, and he mentally nodded agreement.

For one thing, Parthenon had forgotten a piece of advice that Lindquist had given him fifteen years before when Parth was just starting out and both were still riding the rough country. They were fresh from an ambush over in Steeletown where some local citizens had never forgiven the rangers as a whole for interfering in local affairs a few months earlier. 'You see, Parthenon,' Lindquist had said, 'once you have made a place angry, it stays angry.'

Parth had done it again. He had made Flat Rock angry with him, real angry. Those who did not already hate him were bound to become suspicious, wary, sullen around him. Getting much information about Barney Shivers and Golden, who were respected local men, was not going to be easy.

'Here we are,' the Dutchman said, pausing at the door to a second-story room.

'Be careful going through, Papa,' the Dutchman's wife counseled, 'we don't want to crack his poor head again.' That was avoided and Parthenon placed on a freshly made bed with an apricot-colored coverlet, which could hardly have ever been necessary in this country, but brightened up the rather plain room.

'You should have taken that from under him,' the wife said, meaning the bed cover, and set about doing it with Margaret's help.

Lying atop clean sheets on a new mattress, Parthenon found himself comfortable enough, perhaps too comfortable. He found the alertness draining from his body with the loss of blood, and this was no time to pass out.

'Get that doctor,' he said weakly to Margaret, who was hovering over the bed.

'What doctor does he mean?' the Dutchman asked, puzzled.

'I told him about Ike Harmon,' Margaret confessed.

'That whiskey bum!' the wife exclaimed. The Dutchman shushed her. There was no point in sharing their prejudices against the doctor with the patient.

The doctor was obviously half drunk when he appeared in the hotel room, hair tangled, clothing disheveled. Parthenon was in no condition to object, besides, Harmon, as the Dutchman had told him while Margaret was gone, was competent in his way. His experience in Flat Rock, it seemed, was confined to gunshot wounds and the occasional broken bone. He stayed at Placer's where the majority of his practice involved these disorders. He was a patch, plaster, and discharge type of physician which was just the sort of man Parthenon needed at the moment.

Ike Harmon, who wore misshapen steel-rimmed glasses, first demanded the old bandaging be removed. He placed his black bag on the floor next to Parthenon's bed and got to work, muttering as he did so. The bullet, it seemed, had struck Parth high on the chest and proceeded into his shoulder from where it had to be removed. Everything was done quickly and with seemingly skilled dexterity. He rubbed some sort of cream over the wounds, bandaged them and gave Margaret a handful of morphine packets. Then he was gone, probably finding himself in need of a fresh drink.

Propped up in bed on a bolster pillow, Parthenon said, 'Well, that didn't take long.'

'Does it hurt?'

'Like fury,' Parth admitted. Margaret was mixing one of the morphine packets' contents in a glass of water.

'He gets a lot of local practice,' she told him. 'I don't really know how good he is, but there isn't another doctor for a hundred miles.'

Parthenon was not in a position to judge Harmon's work either. He was just happy that the doctor had been called this early in the day. By nightfall Harmon would be well into his cups, and Parth would not have wanted a drunken man with a scalpel in his hands going at it. As it was, he was fairly comfortable, especially after drinking down the bitter medicine. He thought he could sleep well for a while. The problem was, there were things he had to do, and he thought that there might not be much time to do them.

Lou Sessions.

If Parthenon was right, she might well be marked for death. Women did not refuse Barney Shivers without retribution.

'Did you ask about Lou Sessions?' he asked in a muzzy voice.

'Yes, I did,' Margaret responded. Why had she not left Parth's side yet? 'I ran into Dwight Charles while I was asking about Dr Harmon at Placer's. I was at the back door, of course. Women and men of any intelligence do not enter the place.' She sighed, frowned, and went on. 'Mr Charles seemed a little startled to find me there. I told him what I needed and told you wanted to talk with Lou Sessions, but you weren't able to go over there just now.

'Charles told me that Lou had on occasion taken outside work . . . ' Margaret seemed flustered now. 'Anyway!' she snapped, 'he said he'd tell her about you and tell her that he owed you a favor. What kind of favor, I couldn't guess at.'

'Whiskey,' Parthenon mumbled. He

133

was on the brink of sleep and Margaret decided that he needed it. She rose, and slipped from the room.

There was no window in the room, which was fine with Parthenon. He didn't have to worry about anyone taking a shot through it, and only occasional light through the door when someone came to look in on him — which was very seldom. At first the Dutchman and his wife peered in anxiously at their guest, the wife touching his forehead feeling for fever. Then with their hotel to take care of, they quit coming and it was only Margaret he saw.

He awoke once to find her by his bed, spooning some sort of chicken broth into his mouth. He swallowed and asked.

'Why are you still hanging around?'

'Who else is there?' Margaret answered. 'Oh, your lady friend will be over tonight.'

'Lady . . . ?' Parthenon was briefly stumped. 'Oh, you mean Lou Sessions.'

'Yes, that one. Why, have you others around?'

Parthenon was forced to swallow another spoonful of the broth before he could answer. 'No. She's the only one. Hadn't you better go up in the hills and run some men off with your rifle.'

Parthenon had meant that as a joke, but Margaret didn't take it that way. She stood, slammed a soup tureen down on the bedside table and stalked out of the room, fitting her hat on. Puzzled, he watched the door close behind her and lay his head back, thinking of a man who had a good job in the city, knew all the right restaurants and all the waitresses working in them, had a soft bed and good friends and suddenly decided to go back to riding the desert, getting himself shot in the process — all over a sack of sugar.

It was getting late when Lou Sessions made her flurried appearance. The brunette burst into the room with apparent trepidation, her eyes wide and searching. She stuttered to a halt in the

135

center of the floor, her hands held in front of her in a fur muff much too warm for this desert weather. Maybe it was an affectation; perhaps it concealed a weapon, Parthenon assumed the latter. He tried smiling to demonstrate that he was no threat to her. There was some shadowy figure lurking in the hall. Margaret, listening, he assumed, hoped.

'Are you the ranger?' Lou asked in a shaky voice.

'I'm sure you already know that,' Parth answered.

'Yes well, I do, who else could you be in this situation?' Lou seemed to wobble a little and she sat down on one of the wooden chairs, inhaling open-mouthed as if she were trying to calm her nerves with some deep breathing. 'The way it's been for me lately, I'm more than distrustful of everyone — I feel like I'm fighting for my life.'

'Barney Shivers, you mean?'

'Who else would I mean! Of course, Barney Shivers — I feel now like I'm next on his list.'

'Did he tell you anything like that?'

'Not Barney. He doesn't make threats, you know; he just does it.' She grabbed the jug of water on the bedside table, poured a glassful, and drank it.

'Why would he want to kill you, Lou? Surely not just because you won't marry him?'

'I don't know that he wouldn't just because of that. He has already bragged that he and I were to be married, and it would cause him to lose face. Barney Shivers is used to having things his way especially where women are concerned.

'But it's more than that,' Lou told Parth. 'Now I know too much. Barney spent many evenings talking. About himself, of course — he feels he is the center of the universe as all such people do.'

'Shivers told you more than he meant to, is that it?'

'He thought it didn't matter if we were married. I couldn't testify against him then, could I?'

137

'That's what I understand,' Parthenon said.

'Well,' she shrugged, 'I know too much and that's *why* I would never marry him.'

'I see,' Parthenon replied, believing that he did.

'So now, being a traitor in his mind, I have to be silenced,' she said, leaning forward in her chair. 'Barney has the need to brag, to tell everything he has done leading to his control of commerce in this part of the territory, and some of it was pretty rough, I can tell you.'

'You know all about how his operation works?'

'Almost all, I'd say. Barney just couldn't stop talking — about how clever he was.'

'I can see he wouldn't want that spread around.' Parthenon shifted just slightly, trying to relieve the pain in his shoulder. 'Was it just his business that he talked about, Lou? Or did he also tell you what had happened to his wife?'

'I know all about that, Ranger. Every bit of it. One more reason I would never marry a snake like him. What do you want to know about it?' she asked. 'I'd be happy to tell you.'

'You sound as if you have no fear of Barney Shivers now.'

'Oh, I do, Ranger. But not long ago I got in contact with some men who will protect me and get me out of Flat Rock alive. I hope. Friends from the old days over in Flagstaff.'

'Tough men, are they?'

'Their names are Hugh and Anthony Stringwell. Never heard of them? They're tough, all right, in fact they're downright nasty mean — but not in the way our Mister Shivers is. They'll walk up to a man if they feel offended and ask him how he cares to make it right — none of this sneaking around, acting sly, gunning down women in their own homes.'

All of which, in Lou Sessions's mind, Barney Shivers was guilty. It seemed that Lou did not mind the company of tough men so long as they were honest about it.

'You expect these men soon?'

'Not so soon that I'm not remembering to keep my head down. Like your friend, Sally Shields.'

Parthenon didn't see the point in explaining that Sally Shields was hardly a friend of his. Lou did have a point — her position and Sally's were pretty much the same. As was that of Margaret. The women knew too much about Shivers and his operation. He had the need to talk about himself, to build himself up.

How much had his wife Monica known? Enough to kill her over? That murder was supposed to have been so that Shivers could take Lou Sessions as yet another wife, but the fear that Monica would start yakking once she was spurned must have played a part in matters. Parth's thoughts had circled back to that point when Lou Sessions began to tell him about the execution of Monica.

'So one night Barney started telling me — again — that he would soon have a splendid house for me to live in. I could kiss Placer's Dance Hall good-bye.' She sighed. 'I said that he'd already promised me everything, and yet I was still in Placer's.'

'He told me that this time was different. He had set certain wheels in motion, and I could start my packing. I must have looked doubtful. He knew I wasn't anxious to marry a scoundrel like him without some assurances, and rushed on eagerly to explain his plan to me — thinking that his being married to Monica was the only reason I wouldn't say yes to his proposal.'

'He told you all about how he was planning to murder his wife?' Parthenon asked, stunned at the lengths an egotistical man would go to to prove that he was superior to those around him. In the hallway the lurking shadow was closer now. Margaret Havens had inched nearer to hear about Monica's death.

'He had hired Farley Davis and Shinto Greaves for the job, had already given them a part of the money. I had never heard of Farley being involved in anything like this before, but Barney told me that money has changed many a man's perceptions.

'Barney wanted Farley specifically because he had a full head of yellow hair, like Golden Loggins, and he was about the same size. Shinto was a known little sneak who in the dark, masked, could easily pass for Reliance Havens.'

'He wanted to frame those two at the same time as he killed Monica?' Parthenon asked. Lou nodded. In the hallway a woman gasped audibly.

'He is just that kind of man, our Barney Shivers. He said he had no use for Shinto anyway, and he had a long-time grudge against Golden Loggins that he meant to settle. It was no accident that Farley Davis lost his hat in the house on that night — he did, didn't he? Barney told him that he was to do it.'

'He did,' Parthenon told her.

'It was only to show off his yellow hair,' Lou told him. 'Say . . . who is that out in the hall listening? She might as well just come in — it doesn't bother me.' Margaret Havens stepped into the room, her mouth tight. 'Oh, it's you. Have a seat, I'm almost through anyway.'

'I knew that Golden couldn't have been involved in something like that,' Margaret said.

'Because you love him!' Lou laughed. 'That's no protection against the truth. Ask the ranger here; I'll bet he's seen plenty of women who loved a snake.'

'Like you and Barney Shivers?' Margaret asked with some heat. Lou just laughed again and said, 'No, darling, I've been up and down a few paths but I never fooled myself into thinking the man I loved could not be guilty . . . not after the first time,' she muttered and then fell silent. Parthenon knew that was not a story they would ever hear.

'What do we do now, Ranger?' Margaret wanted to know. 'What can we do?'

Lou Sessions rose from her seat, smoothing her skirt. 'That's something for you two to decide. Me, I'm going undercover again in a place Barney Shivers can never find me to wait for the men who are on their way to escort me out of town.'

After Lou had swept silently from the room, Margaret repeated her questions, her eyes intently fixed on the wounded ranger.

'What can we do now?'

Parthenon shook his head. 'We could let Marshal Keyser in on what we know. He might be willing to buck Barney Shivers now.'

'You can't be serious! The law in this town is on Barney Shivers's side. He pays a little better than the Territory does. What has Keyser done about Monica's murder up to now? Nothing at all. Come up with a better idea than that.'

'I suppose I'll have to. All talking to him would likely do is get Shivers certain that you, as well, are conspiring with his enemies. As for me — well, I don't think I could count on my position as an Arizona ranger protecting me. It would just make it more likely that I would be shot myself.'

'Again?' Margaret was smiling ironically.

'Yes, again, and I'm getting damned tired of it! They've had two near misses; they'd like to give it another try, I think. Probably they were just hoping that I'd give it up, turn around and go home.'

'But you won't?' Margaret asked with a little uneasiness in her eyes.

'No, how can I? There's known murderers in this town and I'm a sworn law officer.'

'Then what will you do? I don't know if you've noticed it, being confined as you are, but I think the Dutchman and especially his wife are eager to get you out of here.'

'I've noticed it.' It was a subtle shift in things, only a silence that they maintained now, but silence can speak volumes. They were grateful for the help he had given them, but frightened of what Barney Shivers would do, how this might affect their hotel and the cozy life they had set up for themselves. Parthenon couldn't blame them.

'Where will you go?' Margaret asked. Parth shook his head again. He hadn't decided that yet. He certainly could not go back to his Aunt Lolly's, getting her into the line of fire and exposing Sally Shields's whereabouts. He did know that things were closing in on him rapidly. He had too many enemies in Flat Rock. First and foremost was Barney Shivers. Parthenon now knew the name of two of his hired guns — Farley Davis and Shinto Greaves, who had done the actual killing, if Lou was right — though there must have been a dozen more working for him that Shivers could call on to do his dirty work. Parthenon didn't know exactly where Golden Loggins stood, nor did he understand Reliance Havens's involvement in all of this, but they wouldn't have many objections to seeing Parth eliminated.

There were these and more due to arrive: Hugh and Anthony Stringwell, Lou's friends, who were coming to escort her back to whatever harem she had escaped from. Parthenon had not admitted that he knew these two, but he did. That time there had been some bullets cut loose in both directions. He doubted the brothers had forgotten him. And there was the man in black, Quirt Gaffey — Shivers's bodyguard — to consider. He had already made one attempt at killing Parthenon.

This was getting to be too much. He was pretty well shot up and had no place left to lie down and lick his wounds. He could not stay in some bed anyway, not now that this was about to explode. No, he would just have to take it. Go out there and stand — if he could — and invite any one who wanted to take a shot at him in his private shooting gallery to take a chance at it. He could only promise them that the target would be shooting back from here on.

9

The hideout problem was solved with unexpected ease. Parthenon moved in with Margaret in her desert sanctuary. They were gone from the hotel and from Flat Rock in as little time as it takes to say it. Parthenon felt remiss in not thanking the Dutchman for his hospitality, but that would have to wait for another day. They recovered Parthenon's gray and a bright-eyed little sorrel Margaret rode from the stable and struck out for the wilds. The stableman seemed to give them little thought.

The land around them was all unfamiliar to Parthenon, of course, but Margaret on her sorrel picked her way easily though the tangle of canyons and rough ridges. It took less than an hour's riding before they emerged onto a level, yellow grass shelf of land. Margaret lifted her head, indicating toward the east and Parthenon found himself able to look down on a large white house which he knew without being told, belonged to Barney Shivers. They were practically in Margaret's childhood back yard. They came to the face of a low gray bluff fronted with a tangle of chaparral. Margaret paused her pony and so did Parthenon. Looking up he could see nothing that he had expected. There was a small pouting lip of land overhead, and nothing else. Nodding her head positively, Margaret started on again after first surveying the ground around her. She had apparently been checking the place for any signs of unwelcome visitors. Smart girl.

Margaret called back over her shoulder, 'Your horse can make it up here,' and they began the climb, ascending a narrow path through the crowded nopal, manzanita, and sage. They didn't have far to go; they rode easily to the lip of earth and stone that Parth had seen from below. Margaret's hideout was all but invisible; it was a far cry from the snug little cabin Parth had been expecting.

The dirt and rock had been scraped out of the dugout by hand. It had an Indian feel about it. Across the face of the cave, however, there were planks laid horizontally and roughly fitted to the opening. A large rusty hinge was visible on the boards and a roughly carved doorway.

'Nice and private,' Parthenon said. 'How'd it get here?'

'I built it!' Margaret said with pride. 'My sister Sally helped as much as she was capable of, young as she was. And at one time we had a friendly older yardman named Edgar Stone. He did the sawing and brought the planks over in his cart. We were playing at being Indians a lot then —

'It was a good place to hide out from the constant turmoil down at the house whenever Barney got drunk or just happened to feel like yelling at somebody. Sally couldn't stand it when he

151

started doing that.'

Margaret looked around briefly, perhaps remembering those earlier times, then slipped a bent nail — her 'key' — from her pocket, hooked the heavy door with it and drew it open. They stepped into the dark interior smelling of must and turned earth. There was some arrangement of furniture there, Parth could tell even in the poor light, and when Margaret found a candle somewhere and lit it, he could see one small bed, a small puncheon table, and a few brightly painted boxes used for storage.

'I'm surprised that Sally didn't come up here after the murder,' Margaret said. 'She must have valued comfort more than I ever did. Me, I just wanted to be where no one could ever find me until this was somehow ended and Barney Shivers was dead or gone.' Parth noticed that she did not mention Golden Loggins.

'You were fond of Monica, weren't you?'

'Fond? I loved her; she was my mother as well as Sally's. I can still remember her arriving on the ranch. She was bright and cheerful . . . long before Barney Shivers beat her down with his constant carping.

'I had never realized how much I did need a mother. My own had died when I was still very young.'

'From cholera?'

'So they say,' Margaret answered, turning her face away from Parthenon. He didn't pursue what was obviously a painful point.

The soft, wavering glow of the candle left the room in shadows despite the door having been left open. But there was enough light to find your way by. Margaret guided Parthenon to the bed which was obviously hers, sized for her, holding a lingering scent of the dark-haired girl who had shown a lot of strength in the aftermath of Monica's murder. He thought briefly of Sally Shields. He had not known her well enough to form a real opinion of her character, but that trembling fawn did not seem to have the strength, the determination of her older sister.

Parth wanted to protest but found he hadn't the strength for it. He did manage to mumble his thanks.

'It's all right — you're the one with the bullet holes in you. I can tell that even making the ride up here was difficult for you. You kept slumping in the saddle.'

'Did I?' Parthenon asked around a yawn, then he collapsed on the bed.

'You did! Now stay here and get some sleep. I'm going to try to sneak down to the house and get some food. The cook doesn't mind, and Barney is never home at this time of day.'

Parth thought that sounded like a fine idea, but he didn't respond. He was less than a minute away from a heavy, healing sleep.

There was no light when he awoke. There was a rising moon healthy enough to chase a few of the weaker shadows away, but no candlelight. And no Margaret Havens.

Had she deserted him? Had he somehow walked into a cleverly set plan of her father's or Golden Loggins's?' He stretched out his right arm and levered himself into a sitting position. In the opposite corner of the room, there was a small bundle of blankets which stirred even as he watched it. Margaret was there. She must have been exhausted too.

Slowly settling back into his position under the blankets, he watched the night drift by for a while and then eased his way back into a peaceful sleep.

The sun was low and bright when Parthenon awoke. The door to the dugout stood open. He glanced first at the corner where a stack of neatly folded blankets lay. The girl had gone out again somewhere. Probably to see to the horses, Parthenon thought with a qualm of guilt. He had done nothing for his faithful gray horse's comfort the night before. He stretched his arms carefully, and found himself feeling better, the stiffness receding. But then, he thought, thinking back, he had spent most of the last three days doing nothing but lying up in bed. Time was a great healer in his case.

He sat up in bed which jolted him with a sharp, short-lived headache. He decided he could do without the wrapping on his head now and began untying the skull cap. At least his hat would fit again.

Glancing at the small puncheon table beside his bed he saw a serving tray holding what must have been a nice meal when it was delivered: small boiled potatoes, corn on the cob, greens and a pork chop. All of it looked less than appetizing on this cold morning, but he got to it nonetheless. Everything had held its flavor, though, and was more than appreciated by his deprived stomach. He ate most of it, chased it down with a half cup of cold coffee, and leaned back well satisfied.

Minutes later, a now-familiar form briefly blacked out the rising sun and

Margaret came in to the hideout wearing jeans and a new blouse, dark blue. She had been to the big house again, then. She glanced first at Parthenon sitting up in bed, then at the empty tray beside him.

'That must have been some surprise as breakfast!' she said.

'It didn't bother me or my stomach a bit,' Parthenon replied.

'Well, that's good. I didn't want to wake you to eat last night. I still believed that you needed rest more than anything.'

'I did,' he agreed.

She told him, 'Barney Shivers didn't come home last night; he must be out either looking for, or finding, Lou Sessions.'

'Probably.' Judging from her tone of voice, Parth asked, 'You still don't care for that woman, do you?'

'Not much. It's nothing she's ever done to me; it's just the way she conducts her own life — as if she doesn't give a damn about it.'

'Probably she doesn't,' Parthenon said, 'not really. But it's the way she learned to cope with life somewhere along her back trail. She won't be changing any time soon.'

Margaret seated herself at the foot of the bed and looked levelly at Parth, 'Do you know where she is, Ranger?'

'Not really, but I could have made a good guess about it — if she's still there.'

'What do you mean?' Margaret's eyes were bright and inquisitive, not hostile.

'She told me that she has some friends coming to pick her up and escort her out of town.'

'Hard men?' Margaret inquired.

'Hard enough, according to Lou. The kind that is required for such work.'

'Barney will be furious,' Margaret said.

'From what you've told me it doesn't take much to get him mad.'

'No,' the girl agreed, 'but this is a little different, isn't it — he told Lou just about everything concerning his business, whether she was interested or not.'

'You heard that part, did you? I suppose a person can learn a lot lurking in dark hallways.' Parth smiled just a little, enough to let Margaret know that he was kidding.

'I was out there,' Margaret said soberly, 'because I was trying to keep a watch over you, Parthenon.'

'Oh.' Her remark made him slightly uncomfortable. He supposed he just wasn't used to people caring about him.

'So now you have to make a plan to strike back, don't you?' Margaret said. 'The thing is, you're pretty beat up and much outnumbered. What will you do, send for more rangers to help?'

'I don't think my boss would be willing to let me do that. You see, Margaret, I only got this mission authorized as sort of a personal favor.' True — Gabe Lindquist had exhibited no interest in the case which he called 'the sugar sack folly', and despite the fact that Parthenon's prying had unearthed a dozen pieces of evidence, there was nothing solid yet. Parthenon had possibly made a mistake in going after the heads of the land pirates instead of trying to somehow muster evidence of the enterprise in general — but that was too large a task for one man.

'But you are a captain in the rangers! Doesn't that give you some sort of say over the way things are done?'

'Being a captain doesn't matter much when it comes to policy. I'm just another desk captain largely disconnected from events in the field. The main problem is that I have no hard evidence against Barney Shivers's maneuvers. I'd have to gather a whole lot more than I have now to even consider going to Lindquist with a request for additional men.

'Barney Shivers will get what's coming to him,' Parth went on, 'I have no doubt about that. But it's not as if I had his company ledgers, sworn statements from merchants, and short-line carriers to present to my bosses.'

'What can we do, then?' Margaret asked, looking a little unhappy, a little disappointed in Parthenon.

'Keep going about it in the same way, I suppose. Though it seems like that brings me back to the same point — I kill Barney or he has me killed.'

'But I never wanted . . . ' Her voice broke and Parthenon gawked at the girl. Did she care so much for him after such a short period of time? Or was it just general gloom with the recent death of Monica Shivers and the memory of Margaret's own mother, still recent in memory, the loss of her home and her childhood, the unmasking of her lover, Golden Loggins — it was enough to make anyone cry, Parthenon Downs decided.

'But you won't let matters go?' Margaret asked. She had eased up nearer to him and now held his hand in her own.

'No, of course not,' Parth said, conjuring up a weak smile. 'That's not the way rangers are trained. We finish what we have begun.'

'Then you do have an idea? Paths you can follow?'

'Yes, a few of them, though none is very appealing. I think the first thing I have to do is talk face to face with Barney Shivers. That will involve returning to Flat Rock — and, I'm afraid — dealing with his henchmen. It's not a pleasant idea, but I think I have to do it.'

'It sounds dangerous.'

'They will make it so, but I will speak my piece or have them show me why I cannot. Tonight, I believe, I will make my try. It's up to them whether I speak to Barney Shivers or to the guns.'

'I don't believe you'll have that long to wait,' the rough voice from the dugout door said, and Parthenon's eyes shifted that way to find Quirt Gaffey — Barney Shivers's man in black — standing there, gun in hand.

10

Margaret Havens barely had time to sit up and turn her head toward the doorway when she heard the roar of the gun followed by a second and she was jolted to the floor by a heavy thump against her shoulder. The gunfire echoed inside the belfry of the cave. The air was clotted with gunsmoke. Rock splinters from the wall had struck her face and hands as she fell.

Managing to sit up on the stony floor she brushed at her stinging cheek and then said to the man standing over her. 'You didn't have to hit me so hard.'

'You were right in the way,' Parthenon said. 'I thought you could stand a punch a little better than a .44 slug.'

Rising from the floor, Margaret rubbed at her arm where Parthenon had hit her, driving her out of the line of fire as he drew his own gun. 'That man didn't come for conversation,' Parth said.

'No, I suppose he didn't,' Margaret answered, glancing only briefly toward the crumpled form of the man in black. The shots were still echoing in her ears; her nostrils still burned from the spent gunpowder. She nodded at Parthenon's own Colt, which was still clenched in his hand. 'Pretty quick with that, aren't you?'

'Not really,' Parthenon said, swinging his legs heavily to the side of his bed. 'I heard footsteps on the gravel outside; I had my pistol out before he showed his face.'

'Good thing you did,' Margaret said, coming to sit beside him.

'I'd say so — Quirt Gaffey wasn't going to waste any time telling me what he was going to do.'

'Do you think he was alone?'

'I have no idea; he was known to be a loner. He was Barney's personal body-guard, though, wasn't he? Does that mean that Barney Shivers is on the property?'

'I don't think so. It's way too early for him to leave Placer's.'

'Unless he's found Lou Sessions.'

'Unless he's found her,' Margaret agreed. 'But I don't think he's on the ranch. I think Quirt came to check the place out, found our horses in the barn, or talked to the maid or the cook. They were sworn to secrecy, but Quirt had a convincing way about him.'

'He did. Right now he's only convinced me that we have to get out of here. If there is anyone else around, they're certain to have heard those shots.'

'What are you going to do, Parth? What can you do? Certainly you're not well enough yet to fight them on their terms.'

'No. But I'm not going to let them set the terms. I'll have to make a fight on my own, and if I can't . . . well, I will have tried.'

'You're talking feverishly,' Margaret

said, placing her cool hand on his brow. Her touch was pleasant, soothing; he brushed her hand away. She looked at her hand for a moment, aggrieved. As he rose stiffly and reached for his boots, she asked:

'What can I do, Parth? What do you want me to do?' He looked up and saw a hopeful shimmering in her dark eyes.

'I want you to stay out of sight. Who knows what Barney Shivers might get up to if he thinks there will be a trial.'

'Where . . . ?'

'The only place that I can think of, the only place that makes any sense: ride to my Aunt Lolly's. She already has Sally in her charge.'

'That's just it, she may not want — '

'I know my aunt; she won't object. You might tell her that I appreciate it, though. Say I wanted to leave you there while I take care of some business. She'll know what kind; I've had this job of mine for a long time.'

'Alright,' Margaret slowly agreed. 'Parth — take care of your business, but make sure you take care of yourself as well.'

Parthenon smiled and nodded as he reached for his hat. There was no way he could promise that to Margaret or to anyone else. The graveyards were crowded with men who had made promises that could not be kept.

'Let's get the horses,' he suggested, trying his best smile on Margaret. Her own smile seemed to have broken.

They made their way down the hill and to the barn where his gray and Margaret's little sorrel were stabled up. Both looked bright-eyed, eager to leave their confinement. Along the trail they had come upon a saddled roan, which they assumed Quirt Gaffey had been riding. They led it in as well. Parthenon told Margaret:

'I want you to get away from here as soon as you're saddled. Don't wait for anything, and don't ride a straight trail.'

'Then, you're not going with me that far?'

'No, I don't want anybody who

might be looking to see our two horses together. Just go on; I'll stop at the house and tell the maid and the cook that you are all right. After meeting Quirt Gaffey, they're bound to have been worried, especially if they heard those shots.'

'Good. They'll appreciate hearing that. Lord knows they have little to be thankful for these days.'

Both hesitated for a moment; each of them wondered why. Parthenon decided finally that he had an overactive imagination, or that he was feeling lingering gratitude for the nursing Margaret had done the past few days. He turned sharply and walked away from the barn, leading his gray. Whatever the reason he was feeling as he did, it was no time for indulging such thoughts. There was time enough for thinking on the long trail.

Parthenon considered going first to talk with Golden Loggins again. The town of Flat Rock, after all, was filled with men ready to stop him with a bullet, but Loggins himself might be in town as well, and not at home, and Flat Rock was where the ultimate object of his quest was — the land pirate and serial woman-killer, Barney Shivers.

*　*　*

It was the middle of the afternoon before the ranger, the silver badge on his shirt gleaming, his gray horse plodding heavily along, reached the outskirts of Flat Rock. Its aspect was no different than when Parthenon had last seen it, but there was an indefinable sense of unease, of danger in the air.

It could be that Parthenon Downs was the one bringing these unsettling feelings to town.

He guided his horse toward the marshal's office where he had planned his first visit. He found Samuel Keyser behind his desk, his uneasy eyes studying some sort of legal paper. He started to get to his feet, recognizing Parth, but seated himself again, perhaps

169

disturbed by the hard look in the ranger's eyes. Parthenon remained standing. There was bloody bandaging beneath his torn shirt, the marshal saw.

'I need to talk to you, Keyser.'

'Sit down — though I think I can guess what it's about . . . _who_, I mean.'

'You'd be right, Marshal,' Parthenon replied, remaining standing. Deputy Cather poked his head in from the jailhouse cell block and withdrew quickly, not liking the feeling in the air. 'I mean to take Barney Shivers down tonight, and I'll thank you to stay out of the way.'

'You haven't a thing you can convict him on.'

'Convicting him isn't my job — arresting him on behalf of the Territory of Arizona is.'

'You can't have even enough evidence for that,' Keyser said, looking jumpy. The man obviously didn't have the stomach for bracing Shivers and his men.

'I think I do, for questioning at a

minimum. First of all, as you know Monica Shivers was murdered in her own home by two paid assassins.'

'You can't prove that,' Keyser said.

'There were witnesses,' Parthenon reminded him.

'Two frightened young girls?' Keyser actually grinned. 'You know Barney Shivers wasn't there that night.'

'No, but I'm equally sure that he set it up. I've got people who can attest to that as well.'

'Who could . . . ?' The marshal's grin was gone.

'Perhaps Golden Loggins, for one. After thinking it over, he might not have been too happy about the fact that Shivers was trying to frame him for the killing.'

'Golden would never turn on Barney.'

'No matter, really,' Parthenon said, waving a dismissive hand. 'There's someone else Barney Shivers revealed his whole plan to.'

'You can't mean . . . ?' Keyser's face had tightened.

'It doesn't matter who I mean. The fact is that there's evidence. Now, the point is are you going to hold Barney Shivers for trial?'

'I couldn't — not Barney — you don't know how big a man he is around Flat Rock. He'd have himself busted out of here before I could get the door locked behind him.'

Parthenon stood there a moment in silent contempt, letting his eyes rake Keyser's face and trembling hands.

'That's what I thought you'd say, and that's why I came by here to warn you: if you can't be of any help, stay out of my way tonight, because I'm taking Barney Shivers down one way or the other.'

'When . . . where are you planning on trying this?'

'You can figure that out; just stay out of it. Pull a blanket up over your head and stay indoors.'

'Ranger,' Keyser said in what was nearly a whimper, 'I'm not — '

'No you're not,' Parthenon shot back

before Keyser could finish his statement. 'You're not. You're nothing at all, not even a man. Just stay out of my way!'

Marshal Keyser was still sputtering a response when Parthenon went out the front door, closing it behind him. The sun was still high, though the shadows were starting to lengthen in their creep toward the east. Parth considered taking his horse, but instead left it where it stood as he made his way to the alley behind the marshal's office, which he knew led to his next destination.

There were two workmen and a cluster of flies around the back loading dock of Placer's Dance Hall when Parthenon arrived. He told the first man he met, 'I need to see Dwight Charles. Is he in?'

The man hesitated, eyeing the badge on Parthenon's shirt uneasily, then said, 'I'd guess so. In his office, you know where that is?'

'No,' admitted Parth who had never

set foot inside the building before. The man gave him directions to Charles's office, telling him that he could not miss it, which Parthenon considered to be the poorest encouragement a wandering man could ever receive.

The dance hall was silent, cool, smelling of emptiness except for a few men with their bodies draped across the front bar or sagging in their chairs, which were scattered around the room. A dark, bearded gent with a broom was sweeping up, muttering to himself. There was no dancing going on.

Parthenon mentally apologized to the man who had given him instructions; the office of Dwight Charles was easy to find. It was on the ground floor of the structure, and its door stood wide open. Parth started that way, rapped once on the door and stepped into a small, square room which smelled heavily of applied lye soap.

'Oh, Captain Downs,' Charles said from behind a narrow, pecan-wood desk where three stacked red ledgers rested. 'You made it in before the night's festivities begin in earnest.'

'What time's that start?' Parthenon asked, seating himself. Charles's voice was thick with honey tones as he answered. As Parth had believed from the start, the thin dance hall owner was up from the Deep South — Alabama? — and sort of petted his words as he spoke rather than blurted them.

'About now. When the first man has some money from wages or endeavors unrelated to labor. The other boys will follow him in as if he carried a pocketful of magnets and they were iron shavings.'

'Fills up pretty fast, does it?'

'Very fast, and it's hard to keep the clamps on.'

Parthenon didn't take any time coming to his point. 'Is Barney Shivers here right now?'

'I couldn't say right now,' Charles answered in a tight voice.

'What's that mean? I need to find the man.'

Charles leaned back in his chair and ran his narrow fingers through his pale hair. He sighed, sat up straight again, and answered more directly.

'You might or might not know that Barney Shivers keeps an upstairs room here regularly, whether he's staying overnight or not. Room Three.'

'I guessed as much.'

'I have no particular reason to know if he's in the building or not, unless he's causing a row, or needs something extra.'

'I see,' was all that Parth could think to say.

Dwight Charles grew suddenly intent, his pale eyes searching those of Parthenon Downs.

'Does this concern Lou Sessions?'

'It does,' Parthenon answered with a nod. 'Why did you believe it might?'

Charles muttered something, obviously searching for an answer to the simple question. Taking a chance, Parthenon asked:

'Where is she, Charles? Where is Lou Sessions?'

'Well, she's not here!' Charles said hotly. 'I don't know why you'd think I know where she's gotten to.'

'She was your employee.'

'So what!' Charles exploded. 'These girls — I can't keep track of where they go. They're a traveling breed of women.' His heat expended, Charles leaned back in his chair again. The man looked down at his hands and not at Parthenon, who glanced behind him as someone started a small scuffle in the dance hall, then returned his attention to the Southerner.

'How long have you been in love with Lou Sessions?' Parthenon asked flatly. The dance hall owner seemed like he was ready to explode again, then took a slow deep breath, seemed to give denial up as a bad job, and answered:

'Since the first day she came to me looking for a job,' Charles said in his soft drawl. 'How did you guess?'

'You give it away with your eyes,' Parthenon said quietly. 'Besides who else could she trust in this town? Who else would she feel safe with but the man who had sheltered her all these years? She told you that Barney Shivers had revealed way too much to her since he wanted to marry her, that he was furious, murderous when she refused him — because she wanted to marry you.'

Charles didn't so much as nod his head in acknowledgement of those statements as fact. He did say, 'She did have to be protected at least until those friends of hers could arrive from Flagstaff to see her back there.

'I could have protected her; I could have stood up against Barney Shivers — that's what I told her.' His voice became low. 'We both knew that was a lie. She was a dead woman in Flat Rock.'

'But you've had to hide her out — where, at your house? — until Hugh and Anthony Stringwell can get her safely out of town.'

'That's right,' Charles said. 'I don't like the idea of those two toughs on the long trail with Lou, but she told me that she knew them well enough to trust them. Honestly, Captain, I think the girl decided to leave because she didn't want me to be in danger.'

'You mean if Barney Shivers found out that Lou wanted to marry you and not him, he might decide to have both of you murdered?'

'Of course,' Charles said, himself looking toward the open door as another minor scuffle erupted out in the dance hall. 'And then Barney would be thinking that Lou must have told me all she knew about his activities — which, of course, she had done. She needed someone to talk to about him.'

'Finally he told her about Monica's murder?'

'Yes. After that how could Lou tell him that she was not marrying him? She sneaked away like a thief in the night. Of course I took her in. I thought maybe I could talk her out of returning to Flagstaff.' He wagged his head heavily. 'It was no good, Captain, we

179

both knew I could not rescue her.'

'No, but her next move might prove to be as deadly. Shivers has dozens of men riding for him. If they were alerted to the fact that Lou was riding north, she'd never get through, escort or not.'

Charles did not answer. He sat looking like the most miserable man in God's creation. Parthenon told him sharply, 'I need your help right now.'

'Help?'

The innkeeper looked blankly at Parth as if he had never heard the word before and didn't know what it meant.

'I'm going upstairs. I know you told me that Barney wasn't there, so far as you know, but I have to see for myself. I'm really going to find that man and arrest him if I can.'

'You'd never get him out of town.'

'That seems to be the general opinion,' Parth answered. 'We'll just have to see about that. I'm taking things one step at a time. Right now I want to see Barney Shivers's room and what I would like from you is someone to watch my back. There will be a lot of men in here. Some of them work for Barney; others know that killing me would get them in good with the big man. I'm going up those stairs and I want someone watching down below.'

'Of course,' Charles said, rising. 'I told you once that I owed you a favor. I owe you a bigger one now, knowing that you're trying to do what no one else in Flat Rock is willing to try.'

'She's at your house, right?'

Charles sighed. 'Yes, and that's where I always hoped she'd end up — to stay. Now, I think she means to leave Flat Rock tonight. Those friends of hers from Flagstaff came by to pick up what was left of her belongings. No one challenged their right.'

'Tough-looking, are they?'

'Too tough by their looks to my liking. Too tough to have Lou in their hands.'

'She's the one who asked them to come here — maybe she knows them a little better than we do.'

'I don't think that's it so much as she is that scared of Barney Shivers. I already heard some men talking about his having placed a bounty on her. Ranger, couldn't you get her to stay here in Flat Rock?'

'Not if you couldn't,' Parthenon said.

'That too is because of Shivers,' Charles said. 'She doesn't think I would be able to take care of her if she stays; she thinks that I would be put in danger as well.'

'That's likely,' Parth was forced to agree. 'What Shivers hasn't realized yet is that he, himself, is in serious trouble now.' Charles stared long at Parth before the ranger spoke further. 'I will have the man, Charles. It's just a matter of time now.'

'Can you be sure of that?' Charles asked doubtfully.

'You can bet on it,' Parth told the dance hall owner. 'I may not be the meanest, the fastest man riding this desert, but I can guarantee you that I'm the most persistent. Now, I'm going up to Shivers's room. Can you find someone to watch my back?'

'Sure,' Charles said, giving a low whistle and the wide, dark-bearded man Parthenon had seen sweeping up the main dance hall stepped in. In his hands was not his broom, but a double-barreled shotgun. Perhaps the sight of Parthenon's badge had sent the man after it, thinking his boss might need some help.

'Bobo,' Charles said, 'Captain Downs here wishes to go upstairs. His crossing the floor might cause some commotion — you never know. I need you to stand at the foot of the stairs and see that he's not followed.'

'Sure, I watch him,' Bobo growled, his accent twice as Deep South as Charles's was, like a voice rising out of a swamp.

'You'll be all right,' Charles told Parth, 'let me know if you find anything that needs my attention.'

The dance hall was more lively than when Parthenon had come in. A cluster of men stood around a table in the back of the room, already hooting with the effects of strong drink. Parthenon wondered how a man as apparently cultured as Dwight Charles could live there.

He glanced at the faces of the men he passed, but none seemed familiar. Where were Farley Davis and Shinto Greaves, for example? Placer's seemed to be a second home to them. No matter, Parthenon was just glad that they were not there. He had business to conduct.

Starting up the stairs at the end of the building, he glanced back to see the faithful Bobo standing there with a shotgun in his hands, his dark eyes on the room. Parth knew that there could be a dozen men below who might take a shot at killing him, to curry the wealthy Barney Shivers's favor. There may have even been an underground reward posted for Parth's murder.

The evening faded into muffled silence as Parthenon reached the top of the staircase to find himself standing at the head of a poorly carpeted hallway. Cautiously, he started on his way, striding toward Room Three, where Barney Shivers had resided in weeks past.

Glancing up and down the corridor, Parthenon eased his revolver from his holster and took hold of the brass knob of the door. He turned it slowly, not knowing what to expect inside the supposedly empty room.

The threat came from behind him. Before he could open the door, a heavy tread on the hallway's floor spun Parthenon around to find Bob Brown — Reliance Havens — standing there, pistol in hand.

11

'Hold it, Ranger,' Reliance Havens growled before Parthenon could bring his gun around. Parthenon lowered his pistol just slightly.

'What are you doing here?' he asked Havens.

'The same as you, I imagine,' Havens answered in the same growling voice. 'I'm looking for Barney Shivers. I mean to shoot him dead.'

'My idea is to lock the man up,' Parth said, keeping his own voice cool. Havens was on the ragged edge. His forehead was beaded with sweat and his hand was shaky.

'I like my idea better,' Havens answered. 'But he's not in his room. I've been out here for hours, waiting.'

'You didn't look inside?'

'Nobody came; nobody went,' Havens said defensively.

'He might be inside, passed out, or even dead,' Parth pointed out.

'Have your look then; I'm telling you he isn't in there.'

Parthenon had his look. Turning the knob he went into a small, square room with a sagging bed covered with a rumpled red bedspread and a spindly-legged dresser for furnishings. Parth went to the bureau, looking for anything that might be incriminating or point to where Barney Shivers might have gone. He found nothing but clean imported underwear and a dirty yellow shirt.

'Satisfied?' Reliance, who had been watching, asked.

'Hardly,' Parthenon answered, 'but I see you were right. Shivers is not here. Where would he be?'

'If I knew that, I'd be there,' Reliance told Parth.

Parthenon thought it likely that Shivers was still out looking for Lou Sessions, who would be the chief witness in any case made against him, but Lou was presumably tucked away safely at Dwight Charles's house with two gunmen keeping watch over her. Maybe.

Parth turned toward Reliance, studying the lean man's mournful face. 'You say you're out to kill Barney Shivers — why, after all this time working for the man, or with him?'

'He took one too many steps toward the brink of hell,' Reliance answered somewhat numbly. He sagged onto the unmade bed and lifted his pouched eyes toward Parth. 'You know what the man is.'

'Yes, but so did you when you went to work for him.'

Havens nodded his head. 'Well, I did — and I didn't. I knew he was a thief and a pirate, sure. But I was desperate for work and when he offered me some, I leaped at it. You'd ask why since the man had already stolen my wife from me. I was trying to hold on in my little shanty up along North Fork still. But it was tough going. My wife, Monica, was just folding up, looking ten years older than she was ... and we had a 7-year-old little girl, Margaret.'

Havens took a deep breath before continuing. 'I had gone out to work a small silver claim I had and was gone for two weeks or so. When I came back there was food in the house, Monica was wearing a new dress. She didn't lie to me; she told me she had met a man who wanted to take care of her and the girl.

'What was I to do? I don't remember if we argued or not. I could see that she was right in doing what she did. I had pockets in my trousers with holes in them but that didn't matter because I had nothing to put in them. The child, Margaret, was getting to where she had not even milk and bread to eat,' Havens said, 'and Monica deserved more, all the things Barney Shivers did have, like a roof that didn't leak and a decent diet, which I could not provide.

'Barney Shivers took me aside one night in this very saloon and told me he would hire me on running freight for him. It wasn't part of the agreement for Monica and the child — he already had them — but it was meant to prop me up so that I could live decently. He, he promised, would take care of Monica and my daughter forever, and quite well . . .

'You wonder why a man would do such a thing. I don't have a good answer for you, but all I ever wanted was comfort and a better life for my wife and child than I could guarantee.'

'What happened?' Parthenon wanted to know.

'What happened? You know what happened — Barney set his eyes on another woman he proposed to rescue from her small life, Lou Sessions, and he decided that he would have the woman if it meant killing Monica.'

'Evil, is what I call that,' Parth commented. Havens's face was tight, the muscles in his arms taut.

'Evil. Evil mad,' was Havens's growled answer. 'He wanted to kill my daughter as well; did you know that?'

'I was told,' Parthenon replied. He asked then, 'Whatever happened to Shields — Sally's daddy?'

'I know who you mean,' Havens answered. 'He didn't take to being a freighter and told Barney so, even though his own daughter, a few years younger than Margaret, had gone along with her mother. She had entered into a similar deal with Shivers, and after a few years had died living under his comfort and protection. She caught the cholera, they said back then.

'Old Pat Shields, he caught the cholera himself not long after she passed away. There was a lot of it going around at that time — especially in the area of Barney Shivers. Me, I counted myself lucky. My former wife had a fine home with a wealthy man, Margaret was pampered. And I got to see her just about whenever I wanted; to see her alive and healthy.

'So things seemed fine, until I found out that Shivers planned to kill Monica

— and Margaret — and as a capper for the sordid business, decided to frame two of his long-time partners for the job, by hiring two lookalikes.'

'Using Farley Davis and Shinto Greaves to impersonate you and Golden.'

'Did he not?' Reliance asked of the floor. 'I had no guts. I had sold out my pride, my own life to Satan years before, having even given my wife into the hands of the Devil.'

'You thought you were making the only choice possible.'

'Did I . . . I suppose so, though all those lonesome years I missed Monica and my poor little girl.'

'Margaret still cares for you,' Parthenon said. 'I spoke to her not long ago.'

'Does she . . . ?' Reliance said as if it made no difference now, as if nothing could. 'She thinks she's in love with Golden Loggins,' the old man said. Parth just nodded. She and Sally Shields both. The man must have some outstanding qualities.

'What's Golden thinking of doing now?' Parth asked.

'I've no idea. He got a raw deal himself, didn't he? I mean Barney Shivers telling him that he'd take him in as a sort of partner so they wouldn't be at each other's throats. Of course Barney laid the ground rules, and those gave none of the richer cargoes to Golden. At the time, Golden was happy to get that. He hadn't the men to fight Barney Shivers and didn't wish to anyway.

'Golden is the kind who just waits to see if things get better; he's not a bull-headed fool like you and me, Ranger.' Havens rose to his feet. 'I've waited around here long enough — Shivers isn't coming back.'

'I don't think so either. I guess that leaves us but the one choice — find Barney Shivers and bring him down. When I say that, Havens, I mean to say I'm wearing a badge and have my duty to do. I'm determined to bring the man in alive to see his day in court, if it's possible.'

'I understand. There is one thing, though, Ranger. The man killed my wife, and I'm not wearing a badge. You still want me riding with you?'

'I think so, if you're willing. Two of us have a better chance of bringing the pirate down.'

Havens nodded thoughtfully. Parthenon hoped he wasn't going to have trouble with Havens as well, but as he had said, two of them had a much better chance of finishing the job then a lone man. 'Let's have at it, Mister Brown, while there's still some light in the sky.'

* * *

No one looked long at them as they crossed the crowded dance hall. Bobo saw them to the front door then went to exchange his shotgun for a broom. Dwight Charles stood in the doorway of his office, watching them. Perhaps he wished he were going with them — who knew? He slipped back inside and closed the door.

'What's on Charles's mind?' Havens asked as the two passed out into the cool of the evening.

'Lou Sessions,' Parth replied as they walked across the street to collect their horses.

'It's come to that, has it?'

'Apparently it has been that way for a long time.'

'Poor devil; it must have been killing him seeing her with Barney Shivers.'

'I guess so,' Parthenon said, collecting the reins to his gray horse. 'I suppose you'd know how it feels more than I.'

'I suppose I would,' Havens said as with a grunt he swung aboard his stubby bay horse.

Parthenon was immediately sorry he had said anything as he studied the long, deeply etched face of Reliance Havens. He started to apologize, but decided that would only make things worse.

Side by side they rode their horses out of Flat Rock and onto the desert land beyond.

'Looks like we're headed toward Golden's place,' Haven said.

'I think Shivers might be there. We know he's not in town. He probably plans on Golden and whoever else is around to protect him.'

'If he had gone home, that would leave him alone — except maybe for Farley Davis and Shinto Greaves and his bodyguard, Quirt Gaffey.'

'Gaffey won't be with him,' Parthenon said definitely. His eyes were fixed on the horizon.

'Why not?' Havens asked with surprise. 'He almost always is . . . Oh, I see,' he said breaking out in a smile. 'Was he as fast as was reported?'

'Almost,' Parthenon replied. After that they rode on in silence for another mile.

'You know where my daughter is, don't you, Ranger?' Havens asked from out of the gloom. 'You know where

Margaret has gone.'

'I know,' Parthenon answered.

Havens said, 'But you're not going to tell me, is that it?'

'Not now. We've other business to see to first.'

Havens sighed heavily. 'I suppose you're right. We couldn't take her with us. So long as she's safe, let's get on with what we came to do.'

What they had come to do was to enter a guarded property where an unknown number of armed men would be protecting the killer and prince of thieves, Barney Shivers, from the retribution of the law or that of a wild-eyed unpredictable father with a long grudge. Their plan was hope and faith in the righteous balance of the universe.

And to think Gabriel Lindquist discouraged his desk officers from returning to the field! Saying it was a place where old men went to die. But Parthenon had not turned his back on his noble goal — to make sure a sack of sugar was reasonably priced.

They could see Golden Loggins's neat little place as they emerged from the mesquite grove surrounding it. Parthenon paused for a minute to look over the yard. He was thinking there might be guards posted — two or a dozen; it depended on how many of his pirates Barney Shivers had summoned. Farley Davis and Shinto Greaves were bound to be down there. The two knew by now that they had been implicated in murder — where else would they run? They had to trust to Shivers's cunning and his wealth, hoping either or both was enough to save them all from the hangman's noose.

Parthenon only hoped that the vindictive Barney Shivers had not somehow tracked Lou Sessions to her hiding place at the home of Dwight Charles, and that her escort from Flagstaff had arrived.

'They're in there,' Reliance said in a low voice. His horse twitched its ears.

Otherwise the men and their mounts remained still.

'How many?'

'Who knows? I just saw the corner of a curtain twitch. It could be Shivers by himself, though that seems most unlikely. The man always likes to have others around to do his rough work.'

'I can't see anyone in the yard,' Parthenon said. Reliance was right, of course. It was hard to imagine Shivers making his run on his own, not when he had plenty of men who would welcome an extra payday. Thinking that way, Parthenon began scanning the yard again, more slowly, carefully this time.

'Just look for anywhere a man could be,' Parth said. Reliance nodded. What Parth said could cover a lot of places — the house, the barn, tool sheds, the shelter of the forest, boulders, a hay wagon.

'I believe we'll find them fast ... once we start to approach the house.'

'Too fast,' Parthenon agreed. The place could come to resemble a carnival pop-up target game quickly.

Most likely, Parth thought, there would be a couple of men in the house with Shivers — if he was there at all — and two or three posted outside somewhere.

'What are we going to do?' Reliance asked.

'Start on down.'

'You don't want to circle toward the back?'

'What makes you think that's any safer?' Parth asked with a smile. 'Start that pony of yours on down, and ride with your guns loose.' He paused just long enough to remind Reliance, 'I'm coming here to arrest the man.'

He received no answer, had not expected one. It was clear that Reliance Havens was set on destroying Barney Shivers, given half a chance. Shivers had taken too much from him for Reliance to show any mercy.

They slipped out of the wooded land

and started down the yellow grass slope toward Golden Loggins's house. The bare slope was as good a firing zone as any that could have been devised intentionally by men. Parthenon carried his Winchester loosely across the saddle bow, but his eyes were intent, his jaw tight. A thousand years ago when Gabe Lindquist had still been an active field officer, a group of rangers chasing the killer Chato Chavez and his gang had tried approaching an adobe house sitting alone near Wildwood Springs. The day had been hot, the men weary, the land empty around them. They had ridden to within a hundred feet of the house when the front door was opened and every window suddenly bristled with rifle barrels. A few good rangers were killed that day.

Reaching Golden's yard, Parthenon inclined his head, indicating an instruction and Reliance swung toward the left as Parth aimed his pony toward the right. Their eyes flickered from the low house to the nearby barn, to rocks and trees where a man cold be hiding. No one stirred. Maybe, Parthenon thought, this would go easier than they had imagined.

The sharp crack of a Winchester near at hand shattered that bit of wishful thinking.

Parth rolled clumsily to the side of his horse and gave it an extra nudge with his heel to start the animal moving faster. From the corner of his eyes he had seen the flash of his attacker's gun and he risked a return shot, firing under the gray's neck. The shot at the man who was standing in the barn, missed, but the muzzle flash scorched his own pony, startling the horse enough to throw it off its stride. Parthenon, who had been barely clinging to the horse's neck, was shaken free to hit the ground hard and roll up beside a haystack, which was another of the possible targets Parthenon had marked in his mind.

Fortunately he found no one hiding there and was able to scoot forward and lift himself to his knees as three more rounds were fired from the barn hitting the stack of hay with a whoosh and a slap.

From the far side of the house there was also gunfire. Four shots were fired. From the reports of the weapons Parth knew that there had been a revolver and a long rifle in the exchange. The first had been from a handgun, the next two fired rapidly through a rifle — that of Reliance Havens. There was the accompanying cracking of wood having been split by lead and the following keening moan of a man inside the house. As he lay dying the barricaded man fired off one more wild shot with his pistol, then fell silent.

Parthenon felt sure that Reliance had gotten his man, but there was no way to be certain without approaching nearer to the house. That he was unable to do. His man in the barn continued to fire intermittently — close, almost un-aimed shots. Parthenon's body was stiffening, aching in many spots from old encounters. His skull continued to throb from where the bullet had tagged him earlier. Truthfully, that throbbing pain had continued so persistently that he took little notice of it now.

A fresh spate of gun fire had erupted on the far side of the house. That only meant that Reliance was still alive and fighting — for the time being. How many men were inside the low house? There was no way of telling. Parthenon was doing little to help in the fight where he waited behind the smoldering haystack. He would have to move; he was more than a little reluctant to try it.

Taking in three slow, deep breaths and expelling them, Parthenon rose to a crouched position. Removing his hat, he peered over the crown of the haystack. There was no immediate shot from the barn. He could dart for the house itself or try circling to the back of the barn. He chose the latter. If Reliance could not handle whatever was happening, there was little that Parth could do to help out — unless someone burst out the back door of the house, and he could not see why anyone would risk that.

These thoughts occupied about three seconds of Parthenon's time, then he started across the open space between the hay and the barn where he would be briefly visible to the gunman there. He circled the barn cautiously, the Colt preceding his head as he rounded a corner and came to the back of the white barn where a door stood open!

He eased that way, trying not to let his boots scrape against the ground. He wondered — had his man left or was he waiting there, ready for him? There was only one way to find out.

His back to the sun-warmed wall of the barn, Parth eased his way forward. Distantly, he heard two more shots. These should have come from the house itself, but seemed to be farther away. No matter; not for now. Parth had only one man and one gun focusing his attention. There was no point in delaying his entry. He ducked low, bringing his gun to level. His eyes went from the musty darkness of the barn to the bright rectangle of the open double doors at the front of the barn. He must have made some sound that sharp ears detected, for he saw the clumsy turning of a dark figure across the barn. The man fired once but had not even an actual target to shoot at in the dimness. Nevertheless his bullet came too close to Parth as it made its way past his head to slam into the barn's siding.

The ranger had the silhouette in his sights and triggered off one round, which was all that was needed as the gunman bowed his head as if in respect to the .44 slug. He keeled over and sprawled against the floor, quite dead.

Parthenon recognized the dead man through his mask of blood as the blond, Golden Loggins looka-like, Farley Davis. By all accounts Farley was no killer, but Parthenon felt only the slightest tinge of regret over his death. The man was old enough to know what he was doing — he should have pulled out earlier.

That was one down, two if Reliance had gotten his man as Parthenon believed. How many gunmen were there left in the house? And what if Golden Loggins was to return and throw his weapon and those of whoever might be riding with him into the game? There was only one way to find out.

Parthenon stood and walked out into the sunlight of the thunder-filled day.

12

There was gunsmoke rising in thin tendrils from one of the far windows of the house and a whisper of gray smoke from an untended fire within. Parthenon heard no return fire from the yard beyond, caught no sight of Reliance Havens. Glancing toward the hills beyond the yard he saw no incoming riders arriving hastily, guns in their hands.

There was little point in extreme caution at this juncture. Anyone inside the house would have heard the shots fired in the barn. And so, careful to keep his eyes moving, his pistol clenched tightly in hand, Parthenon risked a direct approach to the side door of the white ranch house. There was nothing to hope for except that Reliance's shooting had been enough to keep the gunmen from risking a dash to escape across the open yard.

Such was not the case. The sun was hot on Parthenon's back. His boots crushed the decomposed granite spread near the house. He glanced once at the cottonwood trees along the creek, once to the lonely, empty sky where a single raven coasted.

There was nothing to be seen in that moment; in the bat of an eye, things changed drastically. With no preceding sounds of activity, the side door to the house was yanked open and a red-faced, furious Barney Shivers appeared there. He took one second to recognize Parthenon Downs and then brought his Colt up to blaze fire. Three hurried, but well-aimed bullets were loosed at Parthenon. The ranger felt his right leg give and he dropped to the ground after firing one wild shot in Shivers's direction.

Parthenon landed hard on his back and the breath was driven from him, his own revolver jolted from his hand. Barney Shivers stood over him, his vicious little eyes glittering with fury and frustration.

'Couldn't leave well enough alone, could you?' Shivers panted. 'I'll have this put on your headstone: 'He Died for a Sack of Sugar'.'

Parthenon saw Shivers lift his pistol, but had closed his eyes again before the final shot was triggered off, the blast echoing in his ears, acrid gunsmoke filling his throat and nostrils with heated residue. His eyes remained closed until he felt the heavy impact of the body falling across his legs. It was Barney Shivers; he had been shot and now lay across Parthenon, his open eyes staring at the yellow sun.

'I know you wanted to arrest him, Ranger,' Reliance said thinly as he hobbled forward from the corner of the house, 'but it seemed like it was time to ignore your request.'

Then with a lopsided grin that held a grimace of pain, Reliance tumbled to the ground himself. He was still breathing when Parthenon scooted that way and managed to pull back the man's jacket and shirt to look at the very nasty looking wound he bore.

'Don't bother yourself none,' Reliance said, looking up into Parthenon's eyes, 'there's nothing to be done for it. I can feel the slug in my lung . . . I just got careless; it must have been Barney Shivers himself who got me as I was circling the house. I just ran out of luck . . . not that I ever had much of it.

'You'll see Margaret again, won't you, Parthenon?'

Parth nodded his head slightly.

'Just tell her I love her. I loved her mother . . . They would have died the way I was keeping them. Just tell her that I tried, but I just wasn't the man I hoped to be.'

'You sure went out like one,' Parthenon said with genuine gratitude, 'and I'll tell her that. I'm sure that she always loved her daddy.'

Those were the last words Reliance Havens ever heard in this world, and it seemed to have formed his mouth into faint smile. Parthenon rose to his feet, dusting off his knees. He glanced toward the wooden hills to the west then started off to find his horse.

There was no telling when Golden Loggins would return and Parthenon did not want to be found among the dead.

★   ★   ★

There was no point in staying around Flat Rock after that. Lou Sessions was gone, presumably to the safety of old company in Flagstaff; Sally Shields and Margaret Havens were safe at Lolly's. The dismantling of Barney Shivers's financial empire would require trained bank examiners and a lot of time — there would be more than one arrest warrant arising out of this complicated affair.

Parthenon filled Marshal Sam Keyser in on the details of what he had done and what he still needed to have done.

Keyser said at one point, 'It would be

nice to have Golden Loggins around. He surely knows much more about Shivers's affairs than anyone else. He could fill in a lot of holes in this business.'

Parthenon nodded. His head still clanged with dull pain. His leg had a chafing hole through it. His right arm was crippled up pretty bad. It was as if cuts and bruises were the only things holding his body together. 'It seems that Golden Loggins has more sense than anyone else,' he said as he rose stiffly from the chair in the marshal's office. 'He must have seen the end coming, and left.'

'You, Parthenon, where are you going?'

'Back to Tucson where it seems I belong. Riding a desk. My boss knew exactly what he was talking about when he told me about men trying to return to the field when they should have known that they were just a little too old, a little too slow.'

'But you did a damn good job,

Parth,' Keyser said, rising to shake hands.

'Did I? Thanks, but I know that Gabriel Lindquist had it right — I was just a little too slow, a little bit too hasty in some decisions. This is a job for the younger rangers,' he told Keyser. 'God bless them; they're welcome to it.'

* * *

The saber of yellow sunlight slicing across the room wedged Parthenon's eyes open and then let them slam shut again. He rolled over protectively, his arm over his eyes, counted to three and then grunted. If the sun was that high, it was time to dress and report. It had taken Parth a while to get to the point that he could easily do that, but on this clear sunny morning, he was able to dress and pull his boots on with only a little discomfort.

In the office he found the usual company wearing desultory expressions. Parthenon limped in and made his way to his small office. Men still smiled their greetings, but for the most part his recent adventure had been already well chewed and digested.

'Your man's come in,' one of the rangers did say. Parthenon only nodded; he wasn't sure who the ranger meant and hadn't the time to puzzle it out. It was left to Gabriel Lindquist to straighten matters out for him.

Lindquist was sitting at Parth's small maple-wood desk, fingers steepled in front of him, wearing half a smile.

'Well he's come in, Parth,' Lindquist said, rising. 'Golden Loggins is in my office — do you want to sit in with us?'

'No, I might find him contradicting himself, or believing that's why I was there and playing too cautious a hand. I've told you the most of it — let him fill in any holes I might have missed and tell it as he will.'

'And that should be plenty; he knows most everything about Barney Shiver's network. He's willing to tell us where the stolen wagons are stored while waiting re-shipment, their patterns and often used trails.'

'He's not going to be arrested?' Parth asked.

'No. That's the agreement we reached with his lawyer. It was a good agreement for everybody. Golden can give us the information we need to break the pirates' back.' Lindquist rose and started toward the door. 'You did the job for us, Parth; you've made it a snap to round up the rest of the hijackers. Let me know when you feel like going into the field again.'

'Just take that idea and smother it, will you? I was wrong to go there this time. I can't expect to have that much luck again. I'm just going to sit here and get used to this office work.'

Lindquist was smiling without it showing. He left the door open on his way out of the office. Before Parthenon could sit behind his desk, he heard footsteps in the hall, and turned to see Margaret Havens standing there, smiling at him. She wore a pink dress with lace ruffles, and stood now with her hands folded before her, studying him with what could only be described as amusement.

'Well,' was all Parthenon could say. 'This is quite a surprise.'

'Well, Golden was summoned up here, and since he had asked Sally to accompany him, it only seemed proper for me to accompany them — they won't be married until tomorrow.'

'Really!' Parthenon said with surprise. 'They're getting married?'

'Sally wanted to take care of business at once. She's always loved Golden Loggins, and wanted his name as soon as possible. Besides, I think she was pretty tired of your Aunt Lolly's house.'

'And you?' Parthenon asked, seating himself on the corner of the desk.

'Well, to tell you the truth, I'm pretty tired of it myself. We're working on selling our house and property in Flat Rock. I thought I might try a little town living for a while, just to see how I take to it.'

'Are you sure you'll like it?'

'No more sure than you are, Parth. What do you say we give it a try for a while and make up our minds later on?'

And that was what they decided to do.